Sabotage !

BLACKIE & SON LIMITED
16/18 William IV Street, Charing Cross, LONDON W.C.2
17 Stanhope Street, GLASGOW

BLACKIE & SON (INDIA) LIMITED
103/5 Fort Street, BOMBAY

BLACKIE & SON (CANADA) LIMITED
TORONTO

G 553

It was a simple matter to observe the state of the
crashed aircraft

SABOTAGE!

By

PERCY F. WESTERMAN

Author of "The Mystery of Nix Hall" "Missing, Believed Lost"

Illustrated by Ellis Silas, F.R.G.S.

BLACKIE & SON LIMITED
LONDON AND GLASGOW

Printed in Great Britain by Blackie & Son, Ltd., Glasgow

Contents

Illustrations

SABOTAGE!

Colin Standish, Chief Inspector of the North-eastern Division of the Royal Air Constabulary, was sitting in his private office at Hawkscar. His desk wasn't littered with documents. There were many of them, but they were all carefully arranged in a way that seemed to convey the fact that Standish had an orderly mind, especially where duty was concerned.

He had just completed the reading of a two-page typewritten document. It didn't seem very interesting, although he had read it carefully, until almost the last paragraph. That, figuratively and literally, made him sit up and take notice.

He touched the push of an electric bell on his desk and waited, drumming his fingers upon the document in front of him, until Sergeant Wyke, his confidential clerk, answered the summons.

It was the fourth time that morning that Sergeant Wyke had been called in. There had been a case of sheep-stealing on the High Moors in Swaledale—a district where the local constabulary were handicapped by the difficult country. This, then, was a matter that would require the use of helicopters, and here the Air Constabulary would be of invaluable service.

The second consultation was in connection with a couple of steeple-jacks marooned on a tall chimney on the outskirts of Bishop Auckland. The appeal for aid had been received just over an hour ago. Under Chief Inspector Colin Standish's orders another helicopter had taken off. Sergeant Wyke, on his third visit to his chief's sanctum that morning, was able to report that a wireless message had been received from the assistant inspector in charge of the helicopter that " operations had been successfully completed ".

That was a secondary reason for Sergeant Wyke's consultation with his chief. There was another matter that might prove to be of a very serious nature. One of the Royal Air Constabulary's pursuit machines—jet propelled—and used for trailing suspicious aircraft, had been reported overdue and missing. There were no definite clues as to where and when it had last been seen. Standish had, there and then, to organize a search.

" You rang, sir? " asked Wyke, saluting smartly—he was in uniform and wearing his cap—as he entered the chief's room for the fourth time that morning.

" Yes, Sergeant! Do you happen to know

where Sub-Inspectors Bradfield and Preston are at this moment? I rang up their quarters but had no reply."

"They've gone over to the repairs and maintenance depot, sir. They informed Sergeant Holly of their intention to do so."

"Very good, Sergeant Wyke. You might ring through to the depot and request them to report here as soon as possible. Show them in directly they arrive."

In less than ten minutes the two junior officers were standing to attention in the presence of their superior officer.

Bernard Bradfield was a tall youth in his late teens. It is not necessary to describe him as well-set-up. If he had not been, he would not have held a junior commission in the Royal Air Constabulary. He was of dark complexion with grey eyes and dark hair.

Philip Preston was shorter by about a couple of inches. His complexion was ruddy, and he had blue eyes, while his hair was so flaxen that it might be taken for white.

They had trained together as helicopter pilots at Bere Regis Aerodrome, in the County of Dorset. As such they had come under the notice of Chief Inspector Colin Standish for the far from inconspicuous part they had taken in solving the mystery of Nix Hall.

The result was that he had been instrumental in bringing them into the Air Constabulary. That was eighteen months ago. After a year at the Staff Training College, they had passed out and, to their great delight, had been posted to Hawkscar.

Had they reckoned upon Standish's influence to push them along—which they did not—they would have been very much mistaken. Their chief never hesitated to bestow praise when it was due; conversely he wasn't backward in telling off any of his subordinates—officers or other ranks—for the slightest signs of slackness or inefficiency.

During their six months at Hawkscar the chums had been engaged in a few minor cases, all but one having been brought to a satisfactory conclusion.

The exception still rankled.

They had been in pursuit of a suspect who, in a high-powered car, was making his way over Blackstone Edge, one of the few passes across the Pennines between Lancashire and Yorkshire. There was every indication of a fog settling down on the high ground; so Bernard, by virtue of his brief seniority, decided to bring the helicopter down upon the moorland road and block the way for the suspect's car.

The car stopped all right!

The driver alighted, produced an automatic and vowed he'd plug both air-cops if they didn't take their perishin' machine up and out of it.

The chums had advanced towards him, one on

either side of the road. The fellow levelled his pistol at Phil. Without a second's hesitation Bernard drew his automatic and shot the suspect's weapon out of his grasp. They then rendered first aid to the arrested man, only to discover a little later on that his automatic was a dummy one!

Of course there was what is often known as a stink about it. It had fallen to Standish to reprimand the culprit. He pointed out that policemen are rarely armed, and then only in a state of extreme urgency. Their protection against armed violence lay in the fact that the law inflicts stern punishment upon criminals resorting to force. Rarely does the murderer of a police officer escape the extreme penalty of the gallows.

" But the redeeming feature of this incident is, Bradfield, that you got your man!"

The chums were not altogether happy when they were shown into their chief's presence. They rather suspected it was in connection with the Blackstone Edge incident.

Standish quickly reassured them.

" Take a pew, you fellows!"

That looked better. The chums seated themselves in two hard, cushionless chairs and waited to know what was coming their way.

" Have you ever seen a rope-walk?" asked Standish abruptly.

" Yes, sir," replied Bernard. " One near Bridport, in Dorset."

"That's good! The chances are that it's the one with which I was acquainted, when I was at Bere Regis Aerodrome. That was a few years before you were there. And you, Preston?"

Phil shook his head.

"No, sir," he replied. "I'm sorry, but I don't know what a rope-walk is."

"Your lack of knowledge in that direction must be remedied," observed his chief. "Your dictionary will tell you that it is a long covered walk or a long building where ropes are manufactured. Actually there is a lot more in it than that, as I hope you will be able to discover before very long. Rope-making with hemp, flax and other vegetable fibres is not such an important industry as it was in the days of our old wooden walls. At Trafalgar, for example, warships didn't have iron or steel cables attached to their anchors. They used ropes up to a circumference of twenty-four inches. Nowadays, though some ropes are still made of fibre, they are chiefly of steel and iron."

The chums listened politely but without much interest to what was virtually a brief lecture upon one of Britain's minor industries. They were, however, slightly curious to know why Chief Inspector Standish had introduced the theme.

They were not to be left in the dark for long.

"You have heard of Sir Montague Corton, of Haxthorpe Hall in the East Riding of Yorkshire?" asked Standish, unable to conceal a grim smile.

They had. Valuable jewels had been stolen from the baronet's home by the late notorious Gerald Scatterthwaite, *alias* Steenie Goldstein, of Nix Hall, Yorkshire. Bradfield and Preston had been engaged by him to take him to various places by helicopter in order to carry out sundry crimes. They were, of course, ignorant of the nature of their engagement at the time. It had been Bradfield who had flown Scatterthwaite to Haxthorpe Hall on the occasion of the burglary.

Then, apparently, Standish changed the subject.

" I'm sending you two away on a month's holiday," he announced. " Ostensibly, that is. Actually you are on duty. I must impress upon you both that you are not to give as much as a hint to any of your colleagues about your mission until after your return."

He did not wait to ask for his listeners' agreement. He took that for granted.

" I'm sending you to Dorset, at the request of the County police officials. There's a spot of trouble to be cleared up and they consider that police officers—air police—from outside the district would be better able to do it. That means you'll be in plain clothes and posing as summer visitors. There will be no necessity or occasion for you to carry firearms!"

" We are not being sent to Bere Regis Aerodrome, sir?" asked Preston, slightly apprehensively. He didn't want to contact his former boss, the branch manager of the south-western division of Inter-British Air Services. They had parted in strained circumstances, and although both assistant inspectors of the Royal Air Constabulary would have liked to blow in upon their former employer—just to let him know how they had bettered their condition—it was, perhaps, wisest to give Bere Regis a wide berth.

"Oh no," replied Standish, "although you may have to visit another Bere, also in Dorset. A duplication of name places in the same county very often leads to misunderstanding—both comical and serious!

"Actually you are to make your headquarters at Brinkwater. That's a few miles from Bridport. Here it is on the map. It is only a small place, that provides labour for the nearby Brinkwater Rope Walk. The manager, a Mr. George Tankerton, will give you all the information you may require. I think you can trust him absolutely. He'll know your rank and that you are officers of the Air Constabulary. I've written him to that effect."

"Can you give us any indication of the nature of the case, sir?" asked Bradfield.

"Yes; sabotage! I'll give you this dossier. You can study it this evening to your hearts' content, though I very much doubt whether you'll be much the wiser! I wasn't after I'd been through it. You'll be ready to leave here by ten o'clock to-morrow morning. You will take

H.104. You should be thoroughly used to that type. There will be no identification marks on it to show that it is an Air Constabulary machine."

The chums exchanged swift, comprehending and appreciative glances. The knowledge that they were to continue to fly put a decidedly different complexion on the matter.

" There's no blind hurry to make Brinkwater," continued the chief inspector. " I wouldn't push the old bus too much, if I were you. I want you to break your journey at Haxthorpe Hall and pay Sir Montague Corton a visit. I've already arranged that for half-past ten."

So the conversation had swung back to Sir Montague. What on earth—or in the air, if it came to that—had the baronet to do with the chums' lengthy flying holiday in Dorset?

Standish glanced at the clock, and then at his watch. A very different matter was nearly due to demand his attention.

" You're probably wondering what Sir Montague has to do with Brinkwater," he went on. " Briefly the position is this: amongst his many official and private interests he is the chief managing director of a large company owning rope manufacturing works in several places in the United Kingdom. Brinkwater is one of them. There have been several cases of sabotage and suspected sabotage there recently. He has put the case in our hands, and it's to be hoped that his confidence will be paid by satisfactory results.

2

That's all for the present, I think—and, by the by, you two!"

" Sir ?"

" If I were you I don't think I'd remind him that it's your second visit you're paying to Haxthorpe Hall!"

With ten minutes in hand Helicopter 104 touched down on the grounds of Haxthorpe Hall almost two years after that memorable night when Bernard and Phil had innocently brought their criminal employer there on his raid upon Sir Montague's jewels.

They had alighted on almost the identical spot. Then it had been a pitch-dark night. The Hall, which was supposed to be the scene of an international conference, had been in utter darkness. Except for the sounds of aircraft overhead and the hollow surge of the nearby river as it tumbled over a weir, utter silence had brooded over the scene.

Now everything was different. The sun shone out of an unclouded sky, beating down upon the weathered grey stone walls and the lead-sheeted roofs of the Hall. The river, too, was not in spate but was flowing gently as a self-respecting river should.

The chums walked towards the Hall, each thinking the same thing, yet keeping his thoughts to himself. They were comparing to-day with that night two years past. They were taking very great care not to mention their previous visit to Haxthorpe Hall to its owner!

A liveried serving man relieved them of their flying coats and helmets.

" Sir Montague is expecting you, gentlemen!" he announced as though, having made the appointment, the baronet might not be awaiting their arrival. " This way, please!"

They were taken into a large, well but plainly furnished room. Sir Montague, who was standing on a hearthrug with his back to an empty fireplace, advanced to greet his visitors.

" And how is Chief Inspector Standish?" he asked early in the conversation. " So far as I know, I have not had the pleasure of seeing him. My father, Sir Rugglestone Corton, was vastly indebted to him over the Amir's Ruby—the famous Atar-il-Kilk. And I am, too. A desperate criminal burgled this house almost two years ago to-day. Luckily he missed the ruby. Somewhat remarkably it was Standish who brought his unsavoury career to an end."

The chums listened to this recital without making audible comment. Sir Montague had been mistaken, as they knew, when he had stated that Standish had brought the *soi-disant* Scatterthwaite's career to an end. Standish had certainly trapped the fellow, but he had shot himself dead with his own pistol.

" And now for this Brinkwater business," continued Sir Montague. " We not only suspect

sabotage. Recent advices from our manager there
—a fine fellow of the name of Tankerton—
George Tankerton—say that there is definite
proof of that. So far no one of the employees is
suspect. Fortunately nothing of a similar nature
has taken place in any of the dozen other rope
factories under my control.

" As you are no doubt aware, the Brinkwater
Rope Walk manufactures mainly hemp ropes.
Now do you happen to know what ' rogue's
yarns ' are? Or, perhaps, I should have said
' were '?"

His visitors had to admit that they were
ignorant on that subject. They had never previously heard of rogue's yarns. It sounded
something like " Confessions of ex-Criminals "
that were appearing in a Sunday newspaper.

" Rope made in certain government dockyards
had a coloured yarn inserted through the entire
length; the idea being that it could be identified
as Admiralty property. It was one form of
precaution against theft.

" Now, in the concern which I control we have
copied the idea of the coloured yarn, not as a
guard against theft, but as a guarantee of our
products. Anyone finding a yellow thread will
know that the rope comes from our works at
Stilby, near Whitby. Those buying ropes from
Brinkwater will find a green yarn in them. Ropes
thus marked should be, like Cæsar's wife, beyond
reproach.

" Unfortunately that, at the moment, is not the case. We've had all ropes tested before they are put on the market. A four-inch one, for instance, has a normal working strain of two and a half tons. We, for testing purposes, increase the strain till the section under test breaks. It takes a five-ton strain to do that.

" Within the last few months our manager, Mr. Tankerton—a man of unimpeachable integrity—has reported at least half a dozen cases of clients, some of them long standing, who have returned ropes as unreliable. Worse than that, any rope that fails to stand up to the work for which it is intended is a menace to efficiency and, indeed, to life and limb. Examination of the rejected ropes had given direct evidence that sabotage is the sole cause."

" But could not the damage be caused by saboteurs after the rope had been delivered, sir?" asked Phil.

" Possibly in an isolated instance," agreed Sir Montague. " But when these complaints come from firms in widely separated parts of the country, it's evident that the miscreant, whoever he is, is at work at the Brinkwater Rope Walk.

" It is in the hope that the criminal or criminals will be detected and brought to justice that I requested Chief Inspector Standish to send you down to Brinkwater."

" It is more than likely, Sir Montague, that as soon as we arrive the culprit will desist from sabotaging, possibly to renew his efforts as soon as we return to Hawkscar," observed Bernard.

"A lot depends upon whether you do or say anything likely to arouse his suspicions, Mr. Bradfield. Remember that although Brinkwater is only a small village it attracts a fair number of visitors during the summer months. In addition to its being a rising seaside resort the rope-making industry attracts a fair number of viewers. Because of this, the miscreant would in all probability, confine his activities to the hours of darkness. I hope you don't object to carrying out your investigations far into the night?"

The chums hastened to reassure the baronet on that point. They had put in a lot of night work while they were at Nix Hall, including their previous visit to the grounds of Haxthorpe; but on that subject they continued to keep their own counsel.

The baronet continued to discuss the situation until he had given the two sub-inspectors all the information at his command.

"Have a glass of sherry before you go," he suggested.

His visitors declined the invitation, Bernard pointing out that policemen—whether of the air or of the ground sort—were forbidden to take strong drink when on duty. Should the helicopter meet with a mishap and they come through alive, one of the first questions put to them at the official inquiry would be whether the pilot at the controls had indulged in liquor immediately prior to the last take-off.

" I quite appreciate that," rejoined the baronet. " I'll come along and see you take-off. Although I do a fair amount of flying, I've never been up in a helicopter. Nor have I seen one at close quarters. There's no objection to looking at a Royal Air Constabulary one, I suppose?"

" There's nothing secret about them," declared Phil. " The official markings have been removed from this one. No one could tell it from a privately owned one."

Sir Montague accompanied them to the spot where they had left their aircraft.

" I must get hold of one like it," he declared, after Preston had briefly run over the helicopter's good points.

" Would you like a flip now, sir?" asked Bradfield. " There's no immediate hurry for us to make Brinkwater. We can do it easily in three hours."

" But there is an immediate hurry," declared the baronet, refusing Bernard's offer. " Who knows, except those on the spot, whether the saboteur was busy last night?"

It was a broad hint for the chums to " get a move on ".

Bernard climbed into the forward cockpit. He was to pilot the helicopter for the first half of the run south. Before Phil could board the aircraft, Sir Montague exclaimed:

" Bless my soul! What's wrong now?"

The chums' first reaction was to give quick glances at the helicopter. Nothing seemed to be amiss. Then they caught sight of someone running across the grass in their direction.

" It's my secretary," declared the baronet. " Now what does he want? Something urgent, I'll be bound."

It was. The secretary, part of whose duties was to handle Sir Montague's correspondence— except those envelopes marked " private "—was hurrying toward the helicopter, and was waving a buff-coloured envelope.

" Anything important, Thornebury?" asked the baronet, although he knew that the question was unnecessary. The secretary would not have rushed out of the house had it been otherwise.

Sir Montague read the telegram aloud. That was one of his little peculiarities, although he did not know it.

It was from the manager of the Stilby Rope Walk near Whitby, to which the baronet had so recently referred in conversation with Bradfield and Preston.

It said: " *Regret to inform you serious accident this morning one man killed four injured*—ROBINS."

" I'll have to go there at once," decided Sir Montague promptly. " You'd better call up the Malton air station for a single-seater. No! On second thoughts: will you two take me to Stilby? I can find my own way back."

It was a direct reversal of his recent decision,
but, as had been pointed out to him, there was no
great hurry for Bernard and Phil to arrive at
Brinkwater.

"Certainly, sir," agreed Bradfield smartly.
"But you should get hold of a leather, fleece-
lined coat—it's pretty nippy in this bus!"

"I'll get yours, Sir Montague," volunteered his
secretary.

Bernard had accepted the baronet's offer, but
a difficulty presented itself. The helicopter was
a three-seater, but the rearmost cockpit was
occupied with the chums' luggage.

Phil would willingly have given up his seat,
but even so, he couldn't make the fifty miles run
to Stilby perched upon a pile of suitcases and
other impedimenta. There would also be the
risk of over-loading and unequal distribution in
weight.

"We can leave our gear here," suggested
Bernard, starting to manhandle the luggage.
"It'll be quite safe, won't it, Mr.——"

"Thornebury," replied the secretary. "Yes,
quite. I'll send someone along to keep an eye
on it."

"I know a better plan than that," rejoined
Preston. "I'll remain here till you return,
Bernard! It shouldn't take much more than an
hour. That will save unloading the luggage."

This suggestion was agreed upon.

A few minutes later—Thornebury having

fetched his employer's flying coat and cap—No. 104 rose almost perpendicularly, and at a safe altitude flattened out on its supplementary journey to Stilby.

" Would you care to look round the Hall?" suggested Sir Montague's secretary, after Preston and he had watched the helicopter until it was almost out of sight. " There are worse ways than that for marking time for an hour."

Phil agreed.

" If I were ten years younger I think I'd like to take up a commission in the Royal Air Constabulary," declared Thornebury, unexpectedly.

Phil successfully concealed his surprise. Was it a chance remark on the secretary's part or did he know that Bernard and he were members of that body?

" I suppose fellows in it have quite a good time," he observed in a casual tone.

" Well, you ought to know, being in it," was Thornebury's astonishing rejoinder.

" How do you know that?" asked Sub-Inspector Preston.

" Considering I handle all Sir Montague's official correspondence, it's not to be wondered at that I am aware you two are commissioned members of the Air Constabulary, and that you are about to proceed to Brinkwater to investigate a case of sabotage!"

Phil felt as if he'd been thunderstruck.

" What's the use of all this secrecy when there

are fellows like Thornebury knocking around?" was his unspoken question.

At this stage of the proceedings there could be no answer.

Meanwhile Bernard Bradfield and the baronet were speeding on their way at a modest one hundred miles per hour.

The pilot was already beginning to doubt whether he had done the right thing by accepting Sir Montague as a passenger, and undertaking a mission outside the one to which he was committed. The Air Police headquarters at Hawkscar lay on the direct route to Stilby. He would have to make a detour, in case other fliers from that station spotted the thinly-disguised helicopter— either from the ground or in the air—and reported its presence to Chief Inspector Colin Standish.

They might call him up by wireless or even try to cut out the helicopter's motor by the numbing Z rays. There was, however, but a slight chance of the latter being put into operation. Since the use of jet engines had become general, the Z rays were helpless to bring down any aircraft except those with the obsolescent magneto-fired motors.

Helicopter 104 still relied upon a magneto to keep her going. Bernard would have to run the risk. He had discarded the combined ear-and-

mouthpiece of his radio. Any attempt on the
part of patrolling aircraft to call him up would
be useless, and the chances were that they would
not proceed to extreme measures.

Sir Montague noticed the detour.

" Why are we off our course?" he asked on the
inter-com. " As we're going we'll be over
Scarborough before we know where we are."

Bernard didn't want to give a lengthy explanation or, indeed, even a short one.

He gave a reassuring wave with his disengaged
arm and pointed somewhat vaguely in the
direction of their immediate destination.

Already in the far distance he could see the
ruins of the famous Whitby Abbey. About three
miles short of it he could make out the chimneys
of the Stilby Rope Walk.

Sir Montague had also spotted them.

" You can come down close to those chimneys,"
he announced. " On this side, that is!"

Bernard could have told him that he knew this
part of the Yorkshire coast, from an aerial view-
point, perhaps far better than he did. He felt
tempted to do so especially as his passenger was
showing signs of nervousness. But he realized
that on this occasion discretion was the better
part, not of valour, but of good manners!

Five minutes later the helicopter made a perfect
landing on a patch of hard clay—residue from a
long-abandoned alum works — within a stone's
throw of the rope-works offices.

Bernard kept the helices just turning. He wasn't going to waste any time for his return journey to Haxthorpe.

Half a dozen men, standing behind a short, thick-set individual, were waiting for the head director to alight.

The stocky and far from prepossessing fellow stepped forward.

" Eh! Ah'm right glad you've come, Sir Montague!" he exclaimed. " It's been a rale bad smash, sitha!"

For some not apparent reason the baronet did not wish Bernard to overhear the conversation.

He waved the manager aside, with a curt " Half a minute, Robins!"

Then, thanking Bernard for his prompt and efficient aid, he added, somewhat pointedly, that no doubt the pilot was anxious to complete his interrupted journey.

Bernard took the hint.

He gave the engine more throttle and once more the helicopter rose steadily.

" So that's Manager Robins!" he thought. " I wouldn't like to trust him farther than I could see him. His eyes are too shifty to my liking. I hope to goodness that Manager Tankerton at Brinkwater isn't of his type!"

He alighted in the grounds of Haxthorpe Hall without incident. Phil came out of the house and ran to rejoin him. He was alone. For some reason, Thornebury had remained behind.

" All O.K.?" asked Phil.

" All O.K.," replied Bernard. " And you?"

Preston gave a wry smile.

" I don't exactly know; but that secretary bird knows who we are and where we're bound for."

" In which case we may as well pack up and report to Standish," suggested Bernard.

" That's what I thought; but we'd better carry on and see how conditions are at Brinkwater. A change is as good as a rest, so they say. By Jupiter, it's nearly half-past twelve already! We'll stop somewhere on the way for lunch. Four o'clock should see us at our destination."

It wasn't so easy as all that.

Aided by a fairly strong following wind, H.104 made good progress—so much so that by one o'clock the airmen were somewhere between Leicester and Rugby. It was about time they found a village large enough to possess a hotel capable of providing a well-earned and appetizing meal.

Suddenly Phil called his chums' attention to something on the ground.

It was another helicopter, showing signs of having sustained a nasty crash. It had fallen in one of a number of large fields, and there did not appear to be a house within a mile of it.

Promptly Bernard checked H.104's forward flight. Then he turned the helicopter into the wind and began to bring her earthwards.

There was no need to alight. From an altitude

of about fifty feet it was a simple matter to observe the state of the crashed aircraft. Her rotor was missing, and one of her landing wheels, flat on the ground, projected several feet beyond the crushed fuselage. The other landing wheel was twenty yards away from the main wreckage. There wasn't a sign of any of her crew.

" Nothing we can do," declared Bernard, without the aid of the inter-com. H.104, her helices doing little more than idling, continued to hover over the crashed machine.

" Nothing. It's outside the Nor'eastern Division. There are no casualties."

" So it seems. Crew probably gone off to get assistance. Let's be getting along."

They did so. About a couple of miles farther on they found that they were approaching a village. It consisted of an ancient, unspoilt church with a squat, battlemented tower, a venerable inn, with gables and oriel windows, a few shops and about fifty houses. Outside the inn and separating it from the macadam road was a small green, bordered by trees. On one side of it were three or four wooden benches. People were sitting there, with mugs on the table in front of them. They weren't drinking. Their up-turned faces were gazing at the descending helicopter.

Evidently they were accustomed to seeing helicopters at close range. There were no signs of apprehension as it decreased its altitude. No

one moved from his or her seat. Everyone continued to stare.

With hardly a bump the machine alighted
plumb in the centre of the green.

The chums alighted.

" Do you know anything about an accident to
an aircraft near here?" asked Phil, addressing a
rubicund, middle-aged yokel.

" No, I ain't," was the reply.   " Wot'll be
wrong wi' yon?"

" Nothing," replied Preston.

" Then why've you come here?" asked the
man.

It seemed like a waste of time to explain
matters to him or to his companions, who were
now making up for lost time by quaffing their ale.

The chums went into the inn and found that
a hot meal was ready to be served in an upper
room.   From where they were seated, they could
keep an eye on their aircraft.

The refreshment-partakers went on drinking.
Occasionally they spoke in loud voices, but their
conversation was not on the subject of aero-
nautics.   Some children on their way to school
stopped to gaze at the stationary helicopter.
None of them went near or attempted to touch it.

Presently, towards the end of the meal,
Bernard touched his chum on his shoulder.

" Look who's arrived on the scene now!" he
exclaimed.

Phil did so.

Approaching the apparently abandoned H.104 was the village constable.

Up to within a comparatively short space of time ago, the village constable made up much of the stock in trade of the music-hall comedian. Usually he was portrayed as being short, stout and with a heavy moustache. His uniform was ill-fitting, his boots sizes too big for his turned-out feet. When he spoke, his dialect was not understandable, except to his neighbours. When he produced his note-book and stubby pencil, it was quickly evident that writing and composition were not his strong points.

This policeman was a product of the present time. He was tall, smart in bearing, clean shaven, and was wearing a collar and tie with his well-pressed uniform. Probably he was bi-lingual— usually using the King's English as spoken in police training schools but the patois of the countryside when speaking to the sons of the soil.

Out came his note-book.

"What do you think he's getting us for?" asked Phil. "As far as we know, there is no notice prohibiting a helicopter from landing on the village green."

"If there were those yokels would have warned us," added Bernard.

"Not they! Hullo! He's examining our luggage. Precious little information he'll get there. Hadn't we better go out?"

They proceeded to do so; but they were

hardly out of the main entrance when an excited male voice called out:

"Hey! What do you think you're doing? You've not paid for your meal!"

In truth they hadn't. The activities of the local police—temporarily at least—put all thoughts of asking for their bill out of their heads.

Bernard paid up. The innkeeper mumbled half-hearted apologies; while the police constable, who could not help overhearing the man's accusations, had fresh grounds for suspicions.

"Which of you is the owner of this machine?" he demanded.

"Neither," replied Bernard.

"What do you mean?"

"Only what I said."

"Then whose is it?"

"That would be telling, my man!" rejoined Bernard, slightly amused and not a little resentful of the policeman's domineering manner.

"Have you your identity cards?" he demanded.

Both airmen simultaneously produced their warrant cards. The effect was instantaneous.

Realizing that he had made an error, the policeman drew himself up, and saluted smartly.

"Sorry, sir!" he exclaimed, addressing Bernard.

"That's all right," conceded the latter. "We all make mistakes sometimes. What's the trouble?"

"Two bright lads have broken out of Borstal,

sir. They pinched—I mean, they stole a helicopter like yours, and haven't been heard of since they got away early this morning."

"Well, we might be the escapees," suggested Phil. "If we are, what was there to prevent us stealing clothes belonging to Air Constabulary officers in mufti, and finding these warrants in the pockets?"

"Lumme! I never thought of that one!" declared the policeman, relapsing into the vernacular. What if these two, claiming to be sub-inspectors attached to the North-eastern Air Constabulary, were in fact the wanted men? There was nothing on their helicopter to suggest that it belonged to the air police. "Do you mind hanging on here while I call up my sergeant?"

That might mean a long delay, even though the constable was in direct touch with his immediate superior by means of a wireless telephone device known as the "walkie-talkie".

"Sorry, no time for that, constable," objected Bernard. "You're on the look-out for two escaped Borstal boys. I think we can put you on their track. Two miles or thereabouts due north from here we saw a crashed helicopter lying in a field. There were no traces of the crew. Perhaps they're gone to seek help; or if they are the wanted lads they're probably hiding close by. After that sort of smash they aren't likely to go very far—unless they've had a lift from a passing motorist."

"Thank you, sir, very much," said the police-man, with another smart salute. "I'll proceed to the spot at once, after I've informed the sergeant of my intentions."

The chums left him trying to call-up the police sergeant. There was nothing more that they could do in the matter, except to fly the constable to the scene of the crash. They had done quite enough already that day in that line!

It had just gone six o'clock before Helicopter 104 touched down at Brinkwater. There had been other minor delays on the way, and by this time Bernard and Phil were ravenously hungry in spite of their heavy and appetizing midday meal.

Accommodation had already been fixed up for them at Sea View House, a boarding establishment kept by a Mrs. Marshbarrow. This was through the recommendation of the rope-walk manager, Mr. Tankerton. He had also suggested that the helicopter could be garaged on the works; but the chums had turned that offer down.

If they were to pose as ordinary summer visitors to the nearby village of Brinkwater, it would give the show away completely if the helicopter were to be kept on the premises of the Brinkwater Rope Walk.

Phil, who had been at the controls, had brought the helicopter down in the firm belief that the rectangle that from the air looked like a tennis court was in the rear of Sea View House—a detached building fronting on the main road, which was separated from the rope-walk by a thick-set hedge.

Close to Sea View House was another and slightly smaller dwelling house; but there was nothing to suggest that its grounds could afford landing space—let alone temporary accommodation for a month—for a helicopter.

At first there was no one about. So silently had the landing been made that it had arrived unheard though not unseen.

The chums were about to carry some of their luggage up to the house when a prim, elderly lady accompanied by a weedy-looking youth came out of the back door of the house.

" Good evening!" she greeted them.

" Good evening, madam!" replied the two airmen in unison. Then there was a pause— rather an awkward one—until she inquired:

" And what might you be wanting? Have you met with an accident?"

" No," replied Bernard, " I believe we've booked rooms here—or rather, they were booked for us."

" Indeed you haven't. We're full up for the whole of the summer!"

" Isn't this Sea View House?"

" No, young man, it is not! That establishment is the one over there."

She indicated the smaller, adjoining house.

" Then we'll shift at once," declared Bernard.

" There's no need for you to do that," replied the proprietress of Peacehaven. " Your machine will be quite all right here for to-night. I really

don't think there will be room for it in the grounds
of Sea View. If you like we can come to a satisfactory arrangement for you to keep it here during
your visit. There is a gate between the two back
premises."

As if to support this statement, the gate in
question creaked as it was being opened, and a
man arrived upon the scene.

He was of medium height, about middle-aged,
and wore a pleasant smile as he addressed the
two airmen.

" My name's Nightingale," he announced.
" Jasper Nightingale. Mrs. Marshbarrow saw
you arrive, and concluded that you had made a
slight mistake. Is that not so, Mrs. Knott?"

" Exactly," agreed the landlady of Peacehaven.
" And I've suggested that it would be to our
mutual advantage if these two gentlemen parked
their machine where it is now."

" I'm sure Mrs. Marshbarrow would not object
to that," declared Mr. Nightingale.

Evidently there was no unpleasant rivalry
between the two paying-guests establishments.

A second man joined the party.

He was about six feet in height with a sun-
tanned complexion. He was hatless, revealing a
thick crop of dark-brown hair. He was wearing
a plus-fours suit.

" Sorry I wasn't here when you arrived," he
declared. " I just went into the village to get
some tobacco before the shops closed. My name's

Tankerton. Excuse me butting in, Mrs. Knott."

So this was the manager of the Brinkwater Rope Walk.

"You must be feeling peckish," he declared, after shaking hands with the two chums. "I've been expecting you since three! Let me give you a hand with your bits and pieces."

"And let me bear a hand too," suggested Mr. Nightingale.

It was certainly a case of many hands making light work. The rear cockpit of H.104 was emptied in almost no time and the procession of four made its way to the front entrance of Sea View, where the new arrivals were greeted by the proprietress.

"I'll be off now," said Mr. Tankerton. "If you want to see me at any time after nine to-morrow, you'll know where to find me."

Nightingale also disappeared although he didn't leave the premises.

Then having been shown their room—a large airy one with two single beds—the new arrivals were taken to a private room where dinner was brought in almost at once.

"Not a bad sort of show," remarked Phil.

"It doesn't look crowded," rejoined Bernard. "That Nightingale fellow seems quite a decent sort, and it was jolly good of Tankerton to look us up. I think I'll like that merchant! Did you notice how he looks you straight in the face when he's talking to you?"

"Now you mention it, I did," agreed Phil.

"There's one thing I don't like about this place," remarked Bernard.

"What's that?"

"The name of the house: Sea View—I ask you!"

There were solid grounds for Bernard's dislike.

Through the open window of the room they could see in the immediate foreground a well-trimmed lawn in front of the house. Then a box-hedge separating the lawn from the road.

Beyond the road was a quick-set hedge cutting it off from the premises of the Brinkwater Rope Walk. Immediately opposite Sea View this hedge was pierced by a gateway from which a well-worn path led to approximately the centre of the quarter-mile shed in which the ropes were made.

There the landscape ended. The roof of the rope-walk cut the rest out entirely. Only from the first and second storeys of Sea View could a glimpse of the English Channel be obtained.

After the chums had finished dinner and the remains of the meal had been cleared away, there was a gentle diffident tap on the door.

"Come in!" invited the chums simultaneously.

The door opened and Jasper Nightingale sidled in.

"Excuse me butting in," he began. "I thought perhaps you'd like some information about Brinkwater. It really is a most delightful place, you know. I presume that this is your first visit?"

The two sub-inspectors agreed that it was so. As for obtaining information about Brinkwater and its inhabitants, they welcomed the idea. Amongst the number of commonplace remarks they were likely to hear, some might be of great value in their quest for the detection of the saboteurs at the rope-walk.

" We were just remarking on the unsuitability of the name of this house," observed Phil. " We certainly can't see the sea from here."

" No, unfortunately," agreed their visitor. " And the rope-walk is years older than this house, so that there never could have been a sea-view except from the upper windows. You see that gate and the path beyond? It's virtually a right-of-way. Each of these houses has three or four keys to the gate. Ours are kept on a hook on the inside of the front door."

" Then where does the path lead to?" asked Bernard.

" To the sea, but first you must cross the rope-walk. As you can observe, all the windows are open to the elements. The door at the end of the path is never locked. There's no reason why it should be since there's nothing that petty thieves could take, and even an expert wouldn't try to get away with a hundred fathoms of stiff new rope.

" Inside the walk, the way down to the shore crosses the ropes in course of making by a foot-bridge, just high enough above the ground for the rope-makers to pass without going on their hands and knees. Then you go through another door on the south side of the building and follow the path right down to the sea."

The chums made a mental note of this description. Perhaps their now acquired knowledge would prove to be of immense value before their " holiday " at Brinkwater was up.

" Of course this isn't Brinkwater proper," continued Nightingale. " It's quite a picturesque little village with a minute harbour, fit only for small boats. Are you fond of sailing?"

" We've done a bit," admitted Bernard modestly.

" You can hire a centre-board sailing boat," observed Nightingale. " The charges are quite moderate. I'm keen on fishing—night fishing especially. Sometimes I hire a boat, but mostly I fish from the beach at the end of our right-of-way."

" What are the people like here?" asked Preston artlessly. " The fisherfolk and the rope-makers, I mean."

" Every man jack of them is as straight as a die," replied Nightingale. " Although I don't know what is meant by a die or whether it should be straight or crooked."

" And what sort of man is Tankerton?" asked Phil indiscreetly. He knew he'd been too inquisitive as soon as his words had left his lips, but already it was too late to recall them.

"George Tankerton? I don't think there's a soul in Brinkwater who would say a word against him. But isn't he a friend of yours?"

"Oh yes, rather," replied Phil. "We've been in communication with him for some time past; but just now was the first time we met him. You see, my friend Bradfield here is a bit of a writing man—an author in a small way. He's writing a book on rural industries and wants to bring in the art and skill of rope-making."

"Then he won't find a better man to put him wise than George Tankerton," declared Nightingale emphatically. "That will satisfy your thirst for knowledge of the inhabitants of this end of Brinkwater—except myself. Perhaps you would care to know why I came here in the first place and what I'm doing here now."

The chums managed not to exchange glances.

They hadn't expected the conversation to include personal details of this nature. Had Nightingale, by some mysterious means, already discovered that Mrs. Marshbarrow's newly-arrived paying guests were in fact police officers called in to investigate cases of suspected sabotage?

"You needn't tell us anything to your discredit, Mr. Nightingale," observed Bernard smilingly.

"It's not so bad as that," rejoined their visitor. "I was advised by my doctor after the war to live somewhere on the south-west coast. I had been an air-raid warden and my lungs were affected as the result. But I am quite cured, so you need have no apprehension on that account.

" I became an ardent sea angler. I am convinced that, contrary to popular belief, salt-laden night air is beneficial to people affected by chest trouble. Strangely enough, I never have a cough except when I stoop for any reason. Then, invariably, well—I cough! Why, I just don't know; but I take good care never to stoop if I can possibly avoid so doing."

The conversation drifted into other channels, and presently Nightingale excused himself. He had to prepare his gear for his projected midnight fishing expedition.

" He looks a harmless little fellow," remarked Phil, when the chums again found themselves alone.

" H'm! I suppose so," conceded Bernard. " He certainly is on the garrulous side. I'm dashed if I can understand why a man of his age—I reckon he's near fifty—should prefer to spend nights on an exposed beach to sleeping in a comfortable bed. I'm supposing that the beds at Sea View *are* comfortable. And there's another thing: how does he get in and out of the house after it's shut up for the night? Tell me that, old son!"

Phil couldn't, but the solution of that problem was soon forthcoming, when Mrs. Marshbarrow looked in to see if her two guests required anything.

" Our front door is never bolted, and Mr. Jasper has a key. We never have burglars down our way. Perhaps they think there's nothing worth stealing. To-morrow I'll provide you with a key just in case you're late back. If you come in as quietly as Mr. Jasper—Mr. Nightingale that is—no one in this house will be any the wiser. Liberty Hall this is, except for a few necessary rules, and my guests don't have to ask what they are!"

Towards sunset Phil suggested a stroll.

" Not this merchant!" protested his companion. " I've had enough fresh air to-day and I reckon you have too. We start business to-morrow. I vote we turn in early."

" I wonder if those two Borstal youths have been recaptured yet," said Phil, stifling a yawn.

" I expect so," opined Bernard. " They generally are collared pretty soon. We'll probably read about it in the morning papers."

Within a few minutes of their turning in the chums were sound asleep. They needed to have no misgivings about the comfortableness of their respective beds.

"Any luck, Mr. Nightingale?" inquired Bernard when they met at breakfast-time.

The amateur fisherman shook his head.

"Absolutely nothing doing," he declared. "Usually I have a few bass or whiting to show for my trouble."

"Trouble?" queried Bradfield.

"I call it trouble when my luck is out. When it isn't you'll be able to count upon bass for breakfast. Prepared and served by Mrs. Marshbarrow they are simply perfection. Not that I have anything to say against eggs and bacon."

"You should try eggs and bacon dished up for breakfast in Yorkshire—in the East Riding."

"Are you from there?" asked Nightingale. "You haven't the Yorkshire accent."

"No," replied Bernard, realizing too late that he had given away another point. "I was in business there. Actually I'm Dorset."

"Dorset's not a bad county," rejoined Nightingale somewhat ambiguously. "Well, I'll be seeing you at lunch."

The chums set out to keep their appointment with the manager of the rope-walk.

There were two ways of reaching their meeting-place. Either they could use the gate opposite Sea View and make their way along the western half of the rope-walk, or they could keep to the main road leading to the village of Brinkwater.

" We'd better stick to the road," suggested Bernard. " The workmen might think it queer —as Tankerton has pointed out—if a couple of strangers, unescorted, entered the works by the gate."

Even though their view of the sea was continuously interrupted by the roof of the rope-walk, the chums enjoyed the walk. The view inland of the countryside appealed to them. Half-way to the entrance to the works, they stopped to watch with considerable interest a mechanical excavator at work—little knowing that the moment would come when it would be of great assistance in solving the sabotage mystery.

Adjoining the road and separated from it by a thick hedge was a wide ditch or dyke. The excavator was engaged in scooping up mud and chalk, at half a ton a time, and depositing it with almost mathematical precision to form a new and higher embankment between the dyke and the rope-walk.

The contrivance was worked solely by a man in an enclosed greenhouse-like arrangement, although there was another man—obviously a foreigner—standing by, though what he was supposed to be doing wasn't clear.

There was a temporary lull in the operations.

The driver having stopped the motive power, leaned out of his cab and, smiling cheerfully, bade the two strangers good day.

" You've a tricky job," commented Phil.

" It's not that bad," replied the man. " Bit monotonous like."

" But interesting, all the same," continued Preston. " Do you ever find anything of value when you're dredging this stuff?"

" Only yesterday I scooped up a couple of skulls—not that they are worth much 'cept to the County Museum. Reckon they were smugglers or perhaps West Country folk murdered by that villain Jeffreys nigh on three hundred years back."

With another smile the man put the machinery again in motion.

The chums continued on their way and presently arrived at their immediate destination—the entrance to the Brinkwater Rope Walk. If anyone should have been in doubt as to the industry carried on there, a large white board displayed that information in big black letters.

The church clock in the nearby village was striking nine as they arrived. Mr. Tankerton was already at the entrance to the works office to greet them.

" Dead on time, gentlemen!" he declared. " I suppose the first thing you'd like to do is to inspect the list of employees. I'll answer any questions relating to them to the best of my ability. Between ourselves, there's not a man I wouldn't trust with my last half-crown!"

" Mr. Nightingale spoke of them in similar terms."

" Did he?" rejoined the manager with a breezy laugh. " That shows our reputation extends beyond the limits of these premises. I hope he gave me a good character? But seriously, these cases of undoubted sabotage are assuming alarming proportions. I'm making a test of a length of cable very shortly. You'll be interested, I know."

Tankerton led the two sub-inspectors into a large wooden building adjoining the rope-walk proper.

In it were three men—all of them approaching the allotted span of life. They were side by side and walking backwards. Each had a bundle of yarn round his waist, looking like an ill-fitting life-belt. As he progressed backwards, apparently twiddling his thumbs in front of his stomach, he twirled the yarn into a long, fine rope.

" They're making cordage," explained the chums' guide. " Using exactly the same process as when this business was started two hundred and fifty years ago. Two of those men have been with us for more than sixty years. Of course, they could have packed up when they were sixty-five, but they prefer to hang on. I don't know where we'll find anyone to replace them."

The next place of call was the testing shed, in

which a section of twenty feet of steel cable was about to be vetted.

This operation did not appeal to the chums to the same extent as if the rope had been a hemp one. The saboteur had concentrated his efforts upon those of the latter kind—at least at Brinkwater. As for the incident at Stilby, that might have been purely accidental.

But, since they were on the spot, there was no real reason why they should not see the test carried out.

The testing apparatus consisted of a couple of grooved drums, about fifteen feet apart. One drum, with a strain indicator, was " anchored " to the bed of a trough by means of strong metal straps. The other was capable of being moved under great power produced by a hydraulic ram. Since a section of only twenty feet was to be tested, the extra length between the drums and including three turns round each was made up by means of a heavier length shackled on to it.

" The wire under test has already stood up to the working strain," explained Tankerton. " That's four tons. Double that should be the breaking strain, but I think it will stand up to nearly nine tons before it parts—— Yes, it's five tons so far!"

Then, without warning, the unexpected happened. The rope suddenly parted, its strands flying apart with a vicious hiss. One part of the rope whipped through the air so close to the two chums that it felt as if it had missed their faces by a matter of an inch or so.

They leapt back, although the danger was over.

Tankerton, who had been standing just behind them, caught Phil by the arm.

" Hurt?" he inquired anxiously. " You might have had your throats slit. Stranded wire can be as sharp as a razor. I warned you to stand back a bit!"

" Did you?" asked Phil, who had already pulled himself together after his narrow escape. " I never heard you."

" I did, but with all this noise going on—well, a miss is as good as a mile. But why that wire should part under a five tons' strain is beyond me. You'd like to carry on?"

" Rather!" declared the chums in unison. They weren't going to show the white feather on account of a narrow miss!

Taking them along the main rope-walk, where hemp ropes of various sizes and up to a quarter of a mile in length were produced, Tankerton came to the wooden bridge over the runway.

" Now you're almost opposite your temporary digs," he announced, telling his listeners something that they had heard before. " The path on the other side leads to the shore. Some people think it's a right-of-way. It's nothing of the sort. It's what is termed an ' accommodation path ' and the use of it is restricted to persons living in Sea View and Peacehaven."

"And what would happen to trespassers?" asked Bernard.

Tankerton looked him straight in the face.

"Something very unpleasant," he replied. "It's decidedly remarkable that we've discovered —by careful measurements—that in three cases of suspected sabotage the flaw in the rope occurred almost directly under this bridge you're standing on. In one there was evidence that two of the strands had been cut through by some sharp instrument. In the others it looked as if corrosive acid had been used to weaken the rope. And now it looks as if someone has been monkeying about with our flexible steel wire rope. Imagine, for example, what might happen if defective wire rope were issued to a British warship."

It required little imagination on the part of either of the chums to visualize the scene. Supposing a warship was hoisting her steam- or motor-pinnace, weighing between twelve and eighteen tons. The boat would be raised by the ship's main derrick until it was well clear of the vessel's superstructure. Then it would be swung inboard before being lowered into its place. Now what would happen if the pinnace were even twenty feet above the warship's deck and the sabotaged wire suddenly parted?

There would be enormous damage to the warship and her equipment. Worse still, there would be loss to life and limb. It was not so much the act of sabotage that mattered. It was the result.

"Well, you have a general idea of our layout, I think," observed Mr. Tankerton at the end of their round. "Now it's up to you—with my co-operation, of course—to solve this string of mysterious happenings. If you want me out of business hours, you'll be likely to find me at my home over there."

He pointed to a tall, somewhat narrow stone-built house about a hundred yards from the works gate and twice that distance from the village. It was three storeys in height and had such a slender appearance that it looked as if a southerly gale would send it crashing in ruins.

"I'd ask you in for a spot of lunch only my wife is away on holiday for a month," continued the manager. "But there's no reason why you shouldn't be my guest for dinner at the Crab and Lobster. It's quite a decent little hotel, and they turn out excellent meals, although I suppose Mrs. Marshbarrow's are above reproach."

"We've nothing to complain about in that direction—yet," observed Phil.

They parted, Tankerton going to his office, while his visitors set off on their way to Sea View for lunch.

The mechanical excavator was silent and motionless. The driver and his mate were eating their dinner. They waved to the chums as if they were life-long friends.

"We look as if we're up against something over this business," remarked Bernard. "I don't

think that any of the employees would be so
foolish as to jeopardize their own interests by
minor acts of sabotage.   There's not a man
employed at the rope-works with less than twelve
years' service.   Some have sixty to their credit.
All of them are married and live in the neighbour-
hood.   Now no man, unless he were of unsound
mind, would commit senseless acts like these,
knowing that if the reputation of the firm's ropes
being unsafe became public property, the business
would go phut and he and his mates would be
out of a job."

   " And as the employees are now situated their
chances of obtaining another in Brinkwater would
be practically nil," added Phil.   " Do you attach
any importance to Tankerton's statement that
unaccountable defects in the ropes occur under
or near the bridge near Sea View?"

   " The finger of suspicion points to one man,"
declared Bernard.

   " Who—Tankerton?"

   " Of course not," replied Bernard emphatically.
" Although we haven't the shadow of proof, it's
Jasper Nightingale!"

The rest of the day passed almost uneventfully, the chums exploring the village and getting acquainted with the lie of the land and with some of the inhabitants of Brinkwater.

Jasper Nightingale did not carry out his nocturnal fishing expedition. Next morning he apologized to the chums for the fact that he hadn't provided them with bass for breakfast.

"That's all right," rejoined Phil. "As a matter of fact we're thinking of hiring the sailing-boat you mentioned the other day."

"Old George Cranston's. Well, you might do worse. You can mention my name to him. That may save you having to pay a deposit. Mind you, I say 'may'. And keep well clear of the Bill!"

"What bill?" asked Bernard, thinking he was being warned against having to make some pay-ment in addition to the hire of the boat.

"Why, Portland Bill. It may look a tidy distance from Brinkwater, but with a stiff breeze and a strong tide you'd be swept into Portland race before you know where you are."

"Can you suggest somewhere we can land?" inquired Phil. "Somewhere not far away."

"Yes; Brandy Hole. It's only a couple of miles this side of Brinkwater. Keep about a hundred yards off shore and you'll be clear of a ledge of rocks that uncover at low tide. When they are covered you'll see broken water to warn you."

On their way to the little harbour the chums encountered Mr. Tankerton, who was on his way to the rope-walk.

"Quite a good idea," he agreed, when they had mentioned they had thought of hiring a sailing-boat. "Old Cranston's a decent sort and his boat—the one he lets out on hire—is sound and seaworthy. Tell the old boy you're friends of mine."

"First Nightingale and then Tankerton offering to stand surety over the boat!" exclaimed Phil, when the manager was well out of earshot. "They both seem anxious to contribute to our entertainment."

They were still some distance from the harbour when they encountered a man walking in their direction. He looked a seafaring man from head to toes and wore a fringe of white whiskers under his chin.

"Be you gen'lemen from Sea View?" he asked, tugging at an imaginary forelock.

"We are," admitted Bernard. "Why?"

"Mr. Nightingale he mentions to oi 'ow you may be wantin' to hire the *Ripple*."

"As a matter of fact we did," agreed Bernard.

" We're on our way down to the harbour now."

" And I'm just goin' along to see Mr. Tankerton up at rope-walk. That don't matter much. I'll come back along of you."

" You needn't trouble," protested Bradfield. " The boat's gear isn't locked up, is it?"

" No, 'tain't, zur. It'll be all in the boat. It'll save me feet not goin' back. When you'm my age——eighty-two come September——you won't want to do more walking than you can help!"

A bargain was concluded on the spot and a ten-shilling note changed hands.

The chums found the *Ripple* without any difficulty. For one thing her name was painted on the stern; for another she was the only centre-board boat of her size in the harbour.

She was lying alongside a low quay. Her mast was already stepped, but the spars and lug-sail, together with the oars and boat-hook, were resting on the thwarts.

It did not take long for the amateur crew to set lug-sail and jib, lower the centre-plate and to ship the rudder. The securing ropes were cast off and the *Ripple* glided serenely to the open sea.

There, with the slight on-shore breeze, they steered a course for Brandy Hole, taking care to keep beyond the irregular line of submerged rocks.

They arrived at their destination in remarkably quick time——so quick that they were doubtful whether it was Brandy Hole. Yet there could be no mistake about it—a semicircular line of cliff, terminating in two abrupt crags; while in the centre of the little bay they could discern the mouth of a cave.

They ran the boat ashore on a falling tide, lowered the sail and went off to explore the cave.

"I don't suppose we'll find any clues to the rope-walk mystery!" declared Phil jokingly.

They didn't. Apart from dried seaweed carried into it by the equinoctial tides the cave was bare. No trippers had been there to scratch their names on the walls. Smugglers in bygone days might have used it as a place of concealment for their brandy casks, but anyone could dig for hours without the slightest chance of finding any evidence that the cave had been used for that purpose.

"What a disappointing show!" exclaimed Bernard. "Come on! Let's get afloat again!"

They began to do so. Then their troubles began.

Bernard, the heftier of the pair, set the mainsail and was giving a final swig to the halliard when it suddenly parted. Down came the yard, giving him a smart crack on the head.

He held up part of the stranded rope. There in the centre was the severed part of a green yarn—the distinguishing mark of rope made in the Brinkwater works.

"We'll pull Tankerton's leg when we get back!" he declared.

" But how are we to get back?" asked Phil.

To an experienced boat-sailer the solution
would be simple: the mast could be unshipped
—no one but a raw amateur would attempt to
shin up the mast of a small boat—and the mainsheet substituted for the main halliard. The
longer part of the broken rope could then be
used as a rough-and-ready mainsheet.

The chums weren't well versed in seamanship.
They didn't teach that at the Air Constabulary
College.

" We'll have to row the boat back," declared
Bernard.

They found the rowlocks and shipped them, but
the oars were padlocked to one of the thwarts by
means of a small galvanized metal chain.

" Well, of all the idiotic botches!" exclaimed
Bernard, rubbing his bruised head. " What did
that Cranston fellow do that for? Now we're in
a fine old mess!"

" We can prise the chain open with one of
the rowlocks," suggested Phil.

The chain, though small, resisted their efforts.
The oars remained tightly secured to the thwart.

Then Bernard threw out a suggestion:

" Why not hoist the jib in place of the lug-sail?"

This they did. It was a ridiculously small
spread of canvas, compared with the other sail,
but it was something—something to enable them
to return.

They stowed the anchor, swung the boat round

till her nose pointed seaward and then heaved her down the shingly beach until she was almost afloat.

Fortunately the boat-hook had not been chained. Its stave was made of stout ash, so that the chums could push the boat into fairly deep water.

Then they discovered that the tide was against them. The *Ripple* wouldn't point so high as formerly, and it took them the best part of three hours to come abreast of the middle of the rope-walk. By then the tide was running its hardest. Tack after tack they made, assisting the boat to come about by means of the stern-grating, used as a rough-and-ready paddle.

" We're losing ground, old son!" announced Phil.

" We certainly are," agreed Bernard. " Hullo! There are people on the beach! One of them is waving to us!"

" You're right!" exclaimed his chum. " And, unless I'm much mistaken, the fellow waving his handkerchief is Tankerton! He's telling us to run the boat ashore."

" But we can't," objected Phil. " There's that reef they warned us against. Some of the rocks are showing above the water. The boat would be smashed to bits and we'd get a thorough ducking —if not something worse!"

" We'll go in there," declared Bernard, over-riding his companion's objections and pointing to a small patch of unruffled water between the line of surf.

He put the helm up. With the wind now brought well on her quarter, the *Ripple* appeared to leap over the waves in spite of being greatly under-canvassed.

At the same time, Tankerton and the two men with him hurried along the beach until they were opposite the gap in the partly submerged reef.

For a brief instant the chums thought that they were not going to make it. In the trough of one of the waves the *Ripple* was within her own length of a temporarily uncovered rock. A moment later she appeared to scrape past another obstruction of the same nature. Then she was in calmer and deeper water.

Her forefoot crunched upon the shingle beach. Before she could swing broadside-on to the waves, Tankerton and one of the men gripped her. The crew jumped out—it meant a soaking up to their waists—and by the united efforts of all concerned, the boat, with her floor-boards well awash, was hauled clear of the waves.

" And what has happened to you?" asked Tankerton, after the chums had thanked him and his men for their assistance. " I saw you through my glasses from my office and guessed something was amiss."

Checking his impulse to put the blame upon Brinkwater manufactured rope, Bernard told him about the padlocked oars.

The chums thought they were not going to make it

" Goodness gracious!" exclaimed Tankerton. " Whatever was old George Cranston thinking about to do an idiotic thing like that?"

He was bending over the boat's gunwale to inspect the chain when he caught sight of the severed mainsheet with its tell-tale green core.

" And you've parted the mainsheet," he continued. " Our rope by the look of it, and we didn't make it yesterday. I should say this piece has been in use for at least a couple of years—— Look here, Simpson: cut along and bring me five fathoms of three-quarters rope and some seaming twine. We'll reeve Cranston a new halliard in a brace of shakes, and one that won't part in a hurry."

The employee went off on his errand. Tankerton called him back.

" You'd better bring a hack-saw while you're about it!" he ordered.

" It's putting you to a lot of trouble," suggested Phil.

" In a way I'm responsible for having recommended that old rascal Cranston to you," declared Tankerton. " Now you'd better clear off to your digs, shift your wet clothes, have tea and then come back here. The tide won't serve till six o'clock. If you start then you'll be back in Brinkwater harbour well by seven."

" It sounds as if friend Tankerton is taking charge of operations," remarked Bernard on their way by the accommodation path to Sea View.

"It's jolly decent of him even though he does sound slightly dictatorial," added Phil.

Half an hour later, having changed into dry clothing and having satisfied their hunger, the chums returned to the beach.

The new halliard had been fitted and the chain securing the oars had been sawn through.

"Quite a tough bit of chain," commented Tankerton, tossing it and the padlock under the stern bench of the boat. "You'd better give it to Cranston and ask him what he thinks he's been doing!"

The tide was now making and settling in the direction of Brinkwater harbour, but the wind had fallen light. In the circumstances it was just as well that the oars could be brought into use.

"Care to come with us, Mr. Tankerton?" asked Phil.

"No, thanks," was the reply. "It wouldn't save me anything. Besides, I'd rather not be there when you tick Cranston off."

Once afloat, the *Ripple* made good progress. The church clock was striking seven when she reached her berth. The old boatman was waiting.

"Thought you'd be back come six, gen'lemen," he observed in tones of mild reproof. "You've kept I a-waitin' for close on an hour."

"We didn't know there was a time limit——" began Bernard, but the old fellow interrupted him.

"Toime limit; what would that be?"

"We should have been back well before six if

it hadn't been for that," continued Bernard, ignoring Cranston's question and pointing to the space under the boat's stern bench. " See this padlock and chain? What was your idea of locking the oars so that we couldn't use them?"

Old George screwed up his eyes. His jaw dropped.

" Oi ain't used no lock an' chain!" he declared. " Never set eyes on 'em afore, an' that's gospel truth."

" Then who could have done it?" asked Bernard.

" No one as oi knows on," replied the boatman decidedly. " P'raps someone did it for a joke like!"

" And there's another thing," continued Bernard. " See that mainsheet?"

" Why, if it ain't a new one!"

" Yes, supplied—free of cost, I believe—by Mr. Tankerton. The other one parted. He said that it was worn out."

" If Mr. Tankerton weren't a gen'leman oi should call him a liar!" declared old George heatedly. " That there sheet oi fitted with my own 'ands, back last Easter Monday. It ain't 'ad a couple o' months' wear. Worn out indeed!"

"Quite a little mystery, my festive," said Phil, as the chums were on their way back to Sea View. "Obviously Tankerton made good the defective mainsheet to save his firm's reputation. You'll remember he took the severed rope away with him."

"What was his idea of stating that it was worn out?" asked Bernard. "And Cranston was positive that it was almost new."

"It's one man's word against another's, and that's all there is to it," rejoined Phil. "But it's the padlock and chain that makes me think. Cranston suggested that someone might have padlocked the oars for a joke. It's a senseless joke, if you ask me! Now, assuming that the old chap's theory is correct: who was the joke played upon? Certainly we weren't the intended victims. Tankerton—even supposing that he would have done such a thing—didn't know we were going out in the boat until this morning. The only person who did know was Nightingale."

"Yes, but we mentioned that we were going sailing as we were about to leave Sea View. He wouldn't have had time to nip down to the harbour and padlock the oars. Besides, what object would he have?"

They left it at that—at least for the time being.

Just as they were about to enter the front gate of Sea View, the raucous hoot of an oncoming car attracted their attention.

A large saloon car was slowing down. Someone behind the windscreen was waving one arm as if he had something important to communicate.

" Botheration!" ejaculated Bernard.

" Same here!" added his chum.

They had recognized the driver of the car as a former colleague when they were serving as pilots at the Bere Regis branch of the Inter-British Airways Company. The chums had good reasons for avoiding Charles Bickerton, and now he had turned up at a decidedly inopportune moment.

He stopped his car, flung the door wide open and, omitting to close it, thrust out his hand in exuberant greeting first to Bernard and then to Phil.

" I knew I couldn't be mistaken when I saw your cheerful mugs, even if you aren't in flying kit!" he declared, with a breezy laugh. " Let me see, it's nearly two years since that old ass Williamson gave you the sack over the Nix Hall business! Didn't you sign on with the jolly old air police? I expect you got fed up with that and found a better job?"

" No, we're still in it," replied Phil somewhat impetuously, for he almost at once realized that on that subject silence is golden.

" And what are you doing?" asked Bernard in an attempt to divert the more or less one-sided conversation into another and different channel. " Still with Inter-British Airways?"

" Does it look like it, old sport? No, I was turfed out. Lost my certificate because I knew my job a jolly sight better than old Williamson. Could I afford to run a car like this on a pilot's screw, I ask you? I reckon I've fallen on my feet, even though I might have broken my precious neck."

" And what are you doing now?" reiterated Bernard.

" I'm a press representative on the staff of one of the best-known and most influential papers in the south and west of England, laddie. That's why I'm down this way. As you know, there's been a lot in the press about sabotage in government and private concerns. There are rumours flying around that something of that sort is going on in Brinkwater. That's why the chief sent me along. I suppose you two fellows couldn't tell me something?"

It was of the nature of a direct challenge.

Bickerton was evidently under the impression —a correct one as it happened—that Bradfield and Preston were still members of the Royal Air Constabulary. He had virtually asked them for information concerning the Brinkwater Rope Walk.

To make matters worse, he was talking in a loud, boisterous voice. The windows of Sea View were wide open. It was a still evening. Anyone in the front room of the house could hardly help hearing what Bickerton was saying.

If only the two sub-inspectors could confer, apart from the ex-pilot, upon their line of action! That in present circumstances was out of the question.

It was Bernard who took the initiative.

" Come for a little stroll, Bickerton, my lad!" he suggested. " Not very far."

" How about my car?"

" We won't leave it out of your sight," said Bernard reassuringly. Then, grasping the pressman's arms, the two chums led him a little way down the road, out of earshot of anyone either in Sea View or Peacehaven.

" Look here, Bickerton," began Bernard earnestly. " We've a confession to make. You've probably guessed what it is already. We're attached to the North-eastern Air Constabulary, and we've been sent here to make inquiries about alleged acts of sabotage at Brinkwater. Now then, if we take you into our confidence, will you, on your part, promise not to mention us in connection with your investigations until such time as the case is solved? We also can promise that you will be the first person, apart from the police, to be given information that will enable you to make a scoop that will turn your colleagues green with envy!"

"Righto!" declared Bickerton. "But for my private information—I'm keeping it under my hat, you understand—what's the position to date? Have you any information to work on?"

"I can tell you this, Bickerton: there have been cases of suspected sabotage; but so far we've absolutely nothing that enables us to detect the culprit or culprits. That is so, isn't it, Phil?"

"That sums up the situation," agreed his chum.

"How long are you staying?" asked Bernard.

"About a week. I haven't fixed up yet. I suppose they can put me up at Sea View?"

"I very much doubt it," replied Phil, perhaps too hurriedly. "I think they are full up. Why not try the Crab and Lobster in the village?"

"Might! I'm frightfully hungry, anyway," declared the reporter.

"Not more than we are," thought Phil.

They walked back to the car.

With a cheerful "I'll be seeing you!" Bickerton slid into the driver's seat and set the car in motion.

The chums went into the house, to be confronted by Mrs. Marshbarrow.

"I've put your dinners back in the oven," she announced. "I heard you talking to a friend of yours, and guessed you wouldn't be in sharp on time."

There was a somewhat strange look on the landlady's face. Perhaps she had learned too much from Bickerton's exuberant voice?

The chums saw nothing of the pressman on the next two days. They met Tankerton, however, and he mentioned Bickerton's appearance in Brinkwater.

" An old acquaintance of yours, I understand," observed the manager of the rope-walk. " I gather he's been sent by his editor to gather information. He'll get none from me!"

" And precious little from us," declared Phil. " At least not until the mystery is solved—if it ever will be!"

" You've no suspicions of anyone?"

" None."

Which wasn't exactly a truthful statement!

" Twelve o'clock, old son!" announced Bernard. " Ready? The house seems quiet."

Phil heaved himself out of the easy chair in which he had been resting for the best part of an hour.

" What's it like outside?" he asked.

" It has been raining a little, but the moon's out now," reported Bernard. " We may have to hang around for hours before Nightingale starts on his homeward way. On the other hand, he may be less than forty-five minutes. It will all depend upon his catch!"

" It's almost a joke," said Phil. " This is the third time he's been fishing by night this week, and so far his catch has been *nil*—unless, of course, he has fish of another fry!"

" If so, that's where we butt in," continued Bernard. " It's agreed, then, that we wait in the rope-walk, within easy distance of the foot-bridge. We'll take no action unless Nightingale does something of a decidedly suspicious nature. Then one of us—whoever spots anything queer —will flash his torch and we'll pounce upon him!"

" And, if not, we'll keep quiet until he's had

more than time to return to the house and turn in. Give him, say, twenty minutes, and then we can follow his example."

" Which will mean that we've wasted more than half of a good night's sleep!"

" But supposing he is trying any of his tricks on the ropes now before he goes on to the beach?" asked Phil.

" That's hardly likely," replied his chum. " But we'd better make sure that the coast is clear before we take up our strategic positions."

Warmly clad—for the night air was decidedly cold for the time of the year—they set out for the expected scene of operations.

Before opening the front door of Sea View they took two keys—one to unlock the gate of the accommodation path, the other to let themselves into the house.

Softly they locked the door behind them. The well-oiled lock hardly made a sound. Their rubber-soled shoes were equally silent as they crossed the tarred road and unlocked the entrance to the works.

So far they had the light of the moon to help them. Inside the rope-walk, it was only the diffused moonlight filtering through the glazeless windows that could be of any assistance. They could just make out the silhouette of the foot-bridge over the walk.

Then commenced their long vigil. They had taken up positions one on either side of the bridge

and about ten yards from it, Phil screening himself behind a couple of barrels while Bernard—
more fortunate than his chum—found a pile of
neatly packed canvas sheets.

The wind continued to moan fitfully. Two or
three times there were heavy showers, enough,
one would think, to make Nightingale bring his
fishing operations to an abrupt close.

They heard the church clock in the village
strike one. Neither of them heard it strike two.
A temporary change in the direction of the wind
was responsible for that. Then after a seemingly
long interval it struck the hour of three.

By now, although they were not able to exchange views, both investigators were feeling
decidedly disgruntled. In about an hour's time
it would be dawn. Supposing Nightingale had
decided to try a different part of the shore for
his fishing? He could have gone there without
having to pass through the rope-walk. He might
at this very moment be slumbering, peacefully or
not, in his room at Sea View.

Then both chums sat up and took notice.

There was the sound of footsteps squelching
through the mud of the outside path. The door
on the seaward side was opening, the rusty hinges
creaking as it did so.

For perhaps five seconds, Phil, who was in the
better position for observation, saw Nightingale
silhouetted against the slanting light of the moon.
He was wearing yellow oilskins and was carrying

his disjointed rod in his left hand. Then the door closed. Phil could only just discern the man's form as he began to ascend the ladder of the bridge over the rope-walk.

A metallic object tinkled on the floor of the bridge; Nightingale stooped and groped, evidently trying to retrieve it.

He was bending low for quite a minute. According to what he had told the chums, soon after their arrival at Sea View, he ought to be seized with a prolonged and violent bout of coughing.

He wasn't coughing! He wasn't even breathing heavily!

A beam of light lit up the kneeling man.

Bernard had turned his torch upon the suspect.

He was convinced that his action was warranted. Either Nightingale had dropped a knife or a razor, with which he had intended to sever some of the strands of the freshly made up rope, or an object which might be something of the nature of a small syringe. Bernard had been shown several of these, during his initial instruction at the air police training college. They had been used by criminally minded persons to dope dogs and horses, while one at least had been used to spray corrosive liquid on fabrics. Obviously there were possibilities in the latter method. Nightingale might, at this moment, be preparing to ruin a perfectly new rope by squirting acid into its core.

The suspect showed no sign of surprise when the rays of Bernard's torch were played upon him. He didn't utter a sound or make any effort to escape.

Somewhat baffled by this seemingly indifferent attitude, Bernard, still keeping his torch directed upon the now motionless but still kneeling man, walked towards the footbridge.

Phil, directing his torch on the ground, to enable him to pick his way, approached from the other direction.

" Hullo, Nightingale!" exclaimed Bernard, trying rather clumsily to address the suspect in a natural voice. " What do you think you're doing?"

" I've dropped my pencil," replied Nightingale in a perfectly matter-of-fact tone.

There wasn't a trace of apprehension—nothing to indicate that the still-kneeling man had been surprised in the act of committing a serious crime.

" Not much chance of finding it in the dark," rejoined Bernard. " Let me have a look."

He raised Nightingale to his feet.

" Hang on to the handrail," he cautioned, as he directed the beam of the torch on and around the place where the amateur fisherman had been standing.

" Nothing here," he declared. " It may have dropped into the trough. I'll see!"

He stepped off the bridge and swung himself over the edge of the long trench in which the ropes in course of manufacture were resting on rollers, each about thirty feet apart.

" Nothing there!" he announced after searching for about a couple of minutes. " I tell you what: Preston and I will look for it by daylight."

Nightingale began coughing. It sounded quite a different kind to the one the chums had previously heard.

" I must have caught cold," he declared.

Bernard was quick to take advantage of this announcement.

" It sounds like it," he agreed. " Look here! We'd better see you back to the house. You'd do well to stay in bed with that cough! We'll be out bright and early—before the men come to work—and find your pencil for you!"

Somewhat to the chums' surprise and relief, Nightingale immediately fell in with the proposal. His lethargic manner and the fact that he hadn't shown any surprise at their sudden appearance had taken the wind out of their sails.

Almost without speaking, Nightingale was escorted back to the house. Then, with a courteous " Good night, and thank you ", he went upstairs to his room.

Having replaced the borrowed keys the chums followed his example, except that they did not at once turn in.

Bernard drew a metallic object from his pocket.

" Here's his pencil-case," he announced. " I took good care to see that he didn't pick it up. I was quite under the impression that it was a syringe filled with corrosive acid. Ha! There's something engraved on it: 'Jasper Nightingale, Esq., a token of regard from the Beckthorpe Angling Society, Xmas, 1931.' Well, we needn't have to turn out to find it for him. My giddy aunt, what a fiasco!"

"What puzzles me is why he took it all so calmly when we pounced upon him," observed Phil.

"It has got me guessing too," added his friend. "Our first report to headquarters will have to be sent off to-morrow. I wonder what Standish will say or think when he reads it. So far we've done nothing—absolutely nothing!"

Nightingale wasn't down to lunch, so, in order to relieve his mind, Bernard went up to his room to restore his gold pencil.

"It was awfully good of you to find it for me," declared the owner.

"Well, we happened to be on the spot," rejoined his visitor lamely.

"So it seemed," remarked Nightingale with a smile. "It's the first time in my life-long experience that I've had two members of the police force to escort me home!"

For some moments Bernard was tongue-tied.

"Where did you get that yarn from?" he asked.

"Yarn?" challenged Nightingale. "It's true, isn't it, that you are two members of the Royal

Air Constabulary? That your headquarters are in Yorkshire and that you're down here with the express intention of detecting acts of sabotage?"

"Mr. Nightingale, your statements are perfectly correct," declared Bernard, knowing that it would be useless and perhaps unwise to refute them. "And now, in confidence: do you know of anyone around here who might be involved in cases of that sort?"

"Mr. Bradfield—or ought I to address you as Sub-Inspector Bradfield?—as you know, I spend a great deal of my time fishing. To enable me to do so I go through the rope-walk frequently and at all hours of the night. I can assure you that I have never seen a suspicious character during the whole of my stay here!"

" It looks more and more of a wash-out as time goes on, old son!" observed Phil, after his chum had told him of his conversation with Jasper Nightingale. " It's a pity that you didn't ask him for the source of his information."

" I doubt whether he would have told me that," replied Bernard. " But, if you ask me, I'd say it was that ass Bickerton."

" But Nightingale hasn't met him—at least, I'm not aware that he has."

" He could and probably did overhear Bickerton gassing to us outside the house until we took him well out of earshot."

" Well, I'll jolly well tax Bickerton," declared Phil. " I grant you he may have been overheard, but he's been gossiping down in the village. Nightingale may have got hold of his information second hand—— Hullo! What's happening now?"

A policeman, riding a bicycle, had stopped outside the gate of Sea View. Why Preston should have jumped to the conclusion that the local representative of the law was calling upon them was a question he couldn't well answer.

The constable might be delivering a summons either to Mrs. Marshbarrow or to any of her paying guests.

But instead of going up the garden path to the front door, he crossed the lawn to where the chums were standing and gave them a really smart salute.

" Well, constable, is there anything we can do for you?" asked Bernard.

" Yes, sir; you are in possession of a helicopter."

" That is correct, constable," agreed Bernard, wondering what was going to happen next. Even had he been a civil pilot, there were no regulations against his landing in the next door garden and leaving the helicopter there.

" Well, sir, can you help us? There's a youngster stranded on Black Rock. The lifeboat couldn't get to him. She'd be too late if she could. In any case she's off her station for overhaul and won't be back for a couple of days. The rock'll be covered in less than two hours. The sergeant thought that if you could fly over the place where the kid is, perhaps you can drop him a rope and haul him into your machine."

" We'll do our best, constable," agreed Bernard. " But we shall want a rope."

" I brought one along," the policeman informed him, pointing to one neatly coiled on the carrier of his machine. " And it hasn't come from our local works!" he added, with the suspicion of a wink. "There's no green strand in that one!"

"Bring it along, then," ordered Bernard.

The chums, without waiting to change into flying kit, hurried to the back garden of Peacehaven, where H.104 had been left in the open for just over a week. They placed the coil of rope in the centre cockpit, clambered on board, saw that the controls were properly set, and pressed the self-starter.

The engine fired immediately. The helices began to revolve and quickly the helicopter left the ground.

They had less than a mile to go to the scene of action. Had they wanted directions these would have been speedily forthcoming, for already there was a crowd of spectators lining the beach, their attention divided between the youth in imminent peril and the rapidly approaching helicopter.

Black Rock, as Bernard and Phil were already aware, was a sugar-lump-shaped mass nearly at the western extremity of the reef upon which the *Ripple* had narrowly escaped destruction when they beached her only a few days ago. All around were detached masses of rock upon which the waves were breaking heavily. It was what is known as a "ground swell", the forerunner of a gale. So far, however, there was very little wind.

No boat, not even a lifeboat, could hope to close Black Rock. The bottom would be stove-in on those jagged outlying ledges. Nor could a rocket apparatus be brought into action. The distance was too great for its extreme range. Even had it not been, the stranded youth could not have carried out the instructions so essential to success.

Phil had made a bowline at the end of the coil of rope. As the helicopter approached the scene of action he opened a trap-door in the floor of the centre cockpit.

That was all he could do until Bernard had brought the helicopter over the stranded youth, at a height of about twenty feet above the flat roof of the rock.

The first attempt was a failure. The looped end of the rope missed the lad by about ten feet, while even the much reduced speed of H.104 was greater than that of the on-shore breeze.

The helicopter, temporarily increasing speed, described a wide circle and approached the stranded boy straight into the wind once more. Its velocity was then reduced until it barely held its own against the breeze.

A cheer went up from the spectators.

Bernard, intent upon the controls, could not see what was happening, but the roar of voices informed him that things were going well.

Phil, on the other hand, was able to watch the youth making his bid for safety. He was more than slightly anxious to know what the boy was going to do. The apparently obvious thing would

be for the stranded youth to slip the loop over his
shoulders and allow himself to be lifted clear of
the ground; but to Phil's great satisfaction he
sat in the bight and clasped the rope, above the
loop, with both hands.

Single-handed, Phil could not haul him up
and through the trap-door in the floor. The
youth would have to dangle until H.104 came
down on or near the beach.

" All secure!" shouted Phil, since there was no
need to use the inter-com.

The whir of the air-screw increased. Gently,
one might say majestically, the helicopter roared
vertically to a height of about a hundred feet.

Then it gathered forward speed towards the
throng of now silent spectators.

The crew of the helicopter realized the import
of that silence. There was the risk of the boy in
the bowline losing his nerve. Then the chances
were that he'd slip out of the sling to crash to his
death upon solid ground.

Phil looked down at the unusual passenger.
He need not have worried, for the youth, dangling
at the end of the rope, was waving to the crowd
below!

Turning head to wind, Bernard checked the
helicopter's forward motion and throttled back
the engine. The helices no longer roared. The
renewed shouts of the throng of excited spectators
could be plainly heard for the first time by
H.104's crew.

Gently the rescuing aircraft dropped earthwards until the boy's feet touched the ground. Agilely he slipped off the bowline. The crowd closed in, some patting him on the back until the policeman intervened and proceeded to give him what is commonly known as a good ticking-off, pointing out that there were notices warning people of the danger of visiting Black Rock on a rising tide.

The youth knew of that warning already. He grinned at the constable in a " You're telling me!" way; then, accompanied by about a score of his school chums, he set off homewards, possibly to change his damp clothes, but more likely to describe to his parents the excitement of his first flight by air! It would be equally safe to assume that he would say nothing to them of his visit to Black Rock—they would hear all about that in due course and through other sources—for all that mattered was the fact that he alone of the seventy-odd boys at Brinkwater Council School had flown by helicopter, even though it was at the end of a rope!

Already the rescuing aircraft had returned to her open-air resting-place in the garden at the rear of Peacehaven.

Somewhat to the disappointment of the crowd on the beach, Bernard did not attempt to touch down. All Phil did was to cast loose the rope for the village constable to retrieve and to give a farewell wave to the onlookers.

On returning to Sea View they were greeted by the proprietress with:

" Did you see anything of the smugglers? I just caught a glimpse of your aeroplane as it went over the rope-walk roof!"

" Smugglers, Mrs. Marshbarrow?" rejoined Phil. " Do you mean bearded men in tarpaulin jackets and leather sea-boots, carrying kegs of brandy? If so, we haven't run across any yet."

" I thought perhaps that when Jenkins called —that's the village policeman—it was to tell you about smugglers. And you belong to the police, don't you?"

" He didn't," declared Bernard, ignoring the direct question. " It was something else. You'll probably read about it in the papers."

Mrs. Marshbarrow left it at that.

" I hope to goodness there won't be anything in the press about what we did this morning," observed Phil, after their landlady had gone to resume her household duties. " If we could get hold of Bickerton we ought to be able to induce him to say nothing to his newspaper."

" We can but try," rejoined Bernard none too cheerfully.

They made a point of calling at the Crab and Lobster with the object of seeing the ex-airman reporter.

They were unsuccessful. The landlord of the inn informed them that Bickerton had left by car immediately after lunch. He had an idea that the reporter was on his way to Exeter. In any case he wasn't returning to Brinkwater that night.

The chums' efforts to stay Bickerton's hand having been so far unsuccessful, they made their way back to Sea View.

As they were passing the offices of the rope-walk Mr. Tankerton came running out to speak to them.

"I see you've been busy this morning," he declared.

"Oh, that!" rejoined Bernard. "Were you on the beach?"

"Yes, but I reckon you were too busy to notice me," replied the manager. "But that's not what I want to see you about."

"Then what?" prompted Phil.

"You sent a young pup—a reporter fellow—along to see me," continued Tankerton accusingly. "I sent him about his business; but not before he'd bragged that he'd been with you, when you were civilian pilots at Bere Regis Aerodrome. And he made no secret of the fact that you are sub-inspectors of the Air Constabulary!"

"He should have known better than to say that!" declared Bernard indignantly. "Unfortunately there are others in Brinkwater who seem to know who we are and why we're here."

"And that being so, there doesn't seem much sense in your being here," rejoined Tankerton, rather pointedly.

"It certainly looks as if the cat were out of the bag," remarked Bernard, after they had parted from the manager of the rope-walk. "Apart from Bickerton letting us down—utter ass that chap—Nightingale knows who we are—thanks also to Bickerton—and by the tone of his voice, the village policeman seems to have some sort of idea as to our identity."

"Perhaps Tankerton wasn't far wide of the mark when he said there wasn't much sense in our hanging on here," said Phil. "Though why he said such a thing puzzles me. After all, we're supposed to be investigating an alleged criminal offence. Neither he nor Sir Montague Corton will be called upon to make any payment on that account."

"I don't think Tankerton meant it that way," continued Bernard. "We may not be able to pounce upon the culprit or culprits, but I think we're acting as deterrents. There hasn't been a fresh case of sabotage at the works since we've been here. The damage to that wire was deliberate beyond doubt, but the corrosive substance had been applied probably a week before we arrived upon the scene."

" I suppose you're right," conceded Phil. " We may put the breeze up any saboteur while we're here, but that's hardly the point. We want to catch him red-handed and put him under arrest—— It's a pity we've missed Bickerton."

" Look here: suppose we clear out of here?" suggested Bernard.

" Why?" asked his companion, puzzled by his friend's prompt reversal of policy. " When— to-day?"

" No, not to-day. We'll let it be known that we're off for a night. Give 'em plenty of warning. Then we'll turn up about one in the morning and lie doggo in the rope-walk—the same old spot as last time. If nothing happens, well, that's just a case of hard luck as far as we're concerned."

The rest of the day passed comparatively uneventfully.

During dinner Bernard remarked to Nightingale that it looked like being a cloudy night and asked whether he thought of going fishing.

" No: not to-night," was the reply. " As a matter of fact, I've a slight cold. I'm turning in early."

Just before eleven Phil expressed his intention of retiring for the night.

" Good enough!" agreed Bernard. " I won't be long before I follow your example. I want to finish writing this letter."

" Then don't waste the midnight oil," rejoined his chum chaffingly. " I don't mind betting I'll be sleeping like a log before you're ready for bed!"

Phil went upstairs quietly so as not to disturb the other people in the house; but just as he was about to pass the room occupied by Jasper Nightingale, the door was flung open.

"Thank goodness you're still up, Preston!" exclaimed Nightingale, who was wearing his pyjamas. "There's a fire in the rope-walk!"

He had gone to bed early, as he had already expressed his intention of doing. He was in the habit of drawing back the window curtains immediately before turning in. He hadn't been asleep more than a couple of hours before he awoke to see a glare coming from somewhere across the road.

He jumped out of bed, coughing violently, and went to the open window and looked out. The rope-walk immediately fronting Sea View was on fire. He was about to raise the alarm when he very nearly cannoned into Preston.

"Get a coat on or even a blanket," advised Phil. "Then telephone the police. They'll call out the nearest fire brigade!"

Leaving Nightingale to take elementary precaution against "freshening-up" his cold, Phil hurried downstairs. It didn't very much matter now how much noise he made.

"Rope-walk's on fire!" he declared.

Quite coolly Bernard looked up from his writing. He pushed the nearly completed missive aside.

"Anyone there?" he asked.

" I don't know," replied Phil. " Nightingale's phoning the police. They'll get hold of the fire brigade."

" Then the sooner the better," rejoined Bernard. " There isn't much we can do, but we'll try."

They switched on the lights in the hall. Then, doing something they had never done before, they invaded the scullery of Sea View and took possession of some empty buckets.

" There's a fire extinguisher hanging by the side of the front door!" declared Phil.

" Don't I know it!" declared his chum. " There's nothing in it. Probably it's been empty for twenty years! Come on! We may not be able to put out the blaze, but we may stop it from spreading."

It was a vain hope.

On entering the building they found that the section through which the right-of-way passed was filled with dense smoke. The footbridge over the trough was well alight. Already the ropes beneath it—those in course of manufacture—were smouldering. It looked as if part of the roof would drop at any moment.

The chums knew that there was a hydrant close to the entrance and the central part of the works. They had discovered that during their previous and unsuccessful vigil. They wasted precious moments before they could find the key regulating the supply of water.

When they did they filled the buckets and hurled the contents at inflammable materials close to the blaze. It might be doing some good in restricting the extent of the fire; but apparently it did little more than add clouds of steam to the already billowing smoke.

The chums hadn't been at it more than ten minutes, when the raucous blast of Brinkwater's fire alarm—the all-clear signal during the raids in the war—could be heard above the crackling of the flames.

By this time other helpers from Sea View and Peacehaven were appearing upon the scene.

Conspicuous amongst them were Mrs. Marshbarrow and her neighbour and friendly rival, Mrs. Knott. They, former Civil Defence members, brought with them a stirrup pump. Unfortunately there was no hose pipe to convey the water, so their well-meaning efforts in that direction were useless. Undaunted, they tackled the blaze with a couple of garden syringes, an effort that helped in no small way to prevent the flames from spreading.

Another fresh helper was the "odd boy" on the staff of Sea View. Wearing an old trench coat—much too large for his spare frame—and a pair of gum-boots (and precious little else), he arrived carrying the empty fire extinguisher. This he proceeded to use, pumping feeble jets of air that, if they did anything at all, served to fan the flames.

Other figures loomed through the smoke—men making their way along the rope-walk from the direction of the offices and store rooms. They were carrying a couple of coiled two-inch fire-hoses.

At first neither Bernard nor Phil recognized the leader of this band of fire-fighters.

It was George Tankerton. By example and precept he was urging his men—most of whom wouldn't see sixty years of age again—to couple up the hoses and discharge a copious stream of water not only at the source of the fire but upon the charred beams and planking of the roof.

After about an hour's work the flames were extinguished. The fire-fighters were able to relax, some of them only temporarily.

" Good show, Tankerton!" croaked Bernard, his throat so parched that he could hardly form his words.

The manager looked him in the face.

" Why, it's Bradfield!" he exclaimed. " You're so beautifully disguised that I didn't recognize you. Look at yourself in the glass when you go back to Sea View, and see for yourself! No joke intended!"

" Bad business this fire," remarked Bernard.

" It is. I wonder who raised the alarm?"

" Nightingale; he would probably have been here but for a heavy cold," declared Phil.

" He's not been fishing to-night, then?" asked Tankerton.

" No; he hasn't been out of the house during the whole evening," replied Phil. " So if you've any idea that he dropped a lighted cigarette end or anything else like that, you can put the idea clean out of your head."

" It was caused by someone using that bridge," asserted Tankerton, pointing to the charred wood-work of the structure.

" Not guilty—either of us!" declared Bernard. " Like Nightingale, we were in the house all the evening. We might, with equal curiosity, ask you what you were doing this evening?"

Bradfield meant the question to be a bantering one. Tankerton, evidently, didn't regard it in that light.

" I was at the Crab and Lobster from seven till I heard the alarm," he replied stiffly. " At least a dozen people can bear me out on that—including your bright friend Bickerton."

" He's back, then?" rejoined Bernard, switching on to a less embarrassing subject.

" Rather!" exclaimed the manager. " And have you——?"

He broke off abruptly to thank some of the helpers from Sea View and Peacehaven who were about to return to their respective beds now that the fire had been extinguished. Then he called out to the group of the firm's employees:

" That'll be all for most of you to-night, lads! Peters, Jones and Medhurst," he continued, naming three of the youngest present, " I'll want you to hang on, just in case there's another flare-up. I'll clear off now, but I'll be back in half an hour with some bottles of cider, a loaf and some ripe blue Vinny cheese!"

He turned and had taken a few steps along the rope-walk in the direction of his home, when he stopped, swung round and called to the two chums just as they were about to return to Sea View.

"Sorry, I was forgetting," he declared. "It's about Bickerton. Have you seen what he's written in the *Evening Monitor*?"

"We haven't," replied Phil.

"Then that's a treat in store for you," declared Tankerton. "I don't suppose there'll be a single copy left at the newsagents; but I'll send someone along with mine some time before noon. That'll make you sit up and take notice!"

For some reason unknown to Bernard and Phil, Tankerton failed to provide them, by noon, with a copy of the *Evening Monitor*, describing the part they had played in the rescue of a youth from Black Rock.

The manager of Brinkwater Rope Walk, Ltd., had excited their curiosity by the vague statement he had made concerning Bickerton's report in the paper; and their failure to see a copy only increased their eagerness to secure one.

Immediately after lunch they made their way in the direction of the village. If the newsagent had sold out—and there was no reason to doubt Tankerton's statement that he might have—they might be able to borrow one from the obliging landlord of the Crab and Lobster.

They had barely passed the mechanical excavator, still engaged in deepening the dyke forming part of the boundary of the rope-walk, and had acknowledged the driver's cheerful and somewhat boisterous greeting, when a peremptory hoot of a motor-cycle horn made the chums look behind them.

It was the reporter, Charles Bickerton, tearing

along as usual as if his existence depended solely upon speed, irrespective of any consideration for other users of the king's highway.

At the risk of being run down, the chums signalled him to stop, a feat that he managed to achieve even though at the last moment they had to jump aside.

With a fearful screeching of brakes, Bickerton brought his borrowed machine to a standstill.

" Hullo, my festives!" he exclaimed boisterously. " Anything wrong?"

" That depends," replied Bernard.

" Later on, then," rejoined the reporter. " There's been an accident on the Longmere cross roads. I've simply got to be there."

" One minute," persisted Bradfield. " That won't make all the difference. The accident isn't happening. It has happened. What we want to know is whether you can put us on to a copy of your yesterday's rag—the *Evening Monitor*, I think it's called."

" Certainly," replied the reporter promptly. " As it happens, I have a copy on me."

He handed Bernard a folded newspaper and was about to restart his motor cycle when Phil chipped in:

" We want to ask you a few questions after we've read the report."

" Reading it will take some time," objected Bickerton. " And I'm in a frightful tear. I'll tell you what I'll do. I'll meet you anywhere you

like in an hour's time. That will give you plenty
of chances to read about yourselves. It should
buck you up no end!"

A rendezvous was arranged outside the lifeboat station. Then the reporter rode off leaving
the chums with the much-wanted newspaper.

They had hardly reached the beach on the
eastern side of Brinkwater when they noticed a
man in an obviously distressed condition staggering towards them. He had evidently been in the
sea more or less fully clothed.

" What's wrong?" asked Phil.

" My two little boys," he gasped. " They are
in a rubber dinghy and they're being carried out
to sea!"

It was an all too familiar story. All round
the coasts of the British Isles tragedies or
semi-tragedies of a similar nature are frequently
occurring—caused by the wholly unsuitable use
of rubber dinghies of a type used by Royal Air
Force aircraft. Admirably suited to their legiti-
mate purpose, they are totally unsuited for pleasure
boating, especially in the charge of inexperienced
children—and even adults.

Drawing very little draught and usually propelled by paddle, they become unmanageable in
even a stiffish breeze. Should the wind be an
off-shore one, the hapless crews are blown out to
sea—and that is where the Royal National Lifeboat Institution plays its part.

In this instance the father of the two children

had, as he had supposed, held the rubber dinghy under control by means of a thin life-line. Somehow the rope parted, and although he dashed through the fairly heavy waves in an effort to reach the dinghy, the effort was beyond his physical strength. He was within an ace of losing his life by drowning.

" We'll get old Cranston to go after them in the *Ripple*," decided Phil.

The chums ran towards the harbour, the father of the missing children lumbering along well in their wake.

Cranston, when appealed to, shook his head.

" Tes just gone low watter," he explained. " *Ripple* she be 'ard an' fast aground. There'll be no shifting she until tide makes for another couple of hours. Best call out lifeboat."

" How's that done?" asked Bernard.

" I'll show 'ee," replied Cranston. " I be one of t' crew."

They hurried to the lifeboat shed. The large double doors were closed, but there was a small one giving access to the building.

The old boatman went in, quickly to reappear with something that looked like an old-time blunderbuss. It was a Verey pistol.

Usually lifeboatmen are summoned by firing a rocket, but when they live in a comparatively small area, a Verey pistol is more than sufficient for the job.

Holding the device upwards at arm's length——

it can hardly be termed a weapon although it could inflict a very nasty and perhaps fatal wound —old Cranston pressed the trigger.

Up soared the rocket-like charge to explode with a loud report about two hundred feet in the air.

" Just you take the time afore the crew's ready," advised the boatman.

They hadn't long to wait. Within a matter of minutes, men, most of them well past middle age, were hurrying to man the lifeboat, even as their contemporaries and their predecessors had done and were doing during a period of nearly one hundred and thirty years, to go to the rescue, in fair weather or foul, of those who " go down to the sea in ships ", even though some of those " ships " might be rubber dinghies.

On the face of things this operation would be an easy one: picking up a couple of youngsters adrift in a frail cockle-shell, and returning them to their anxious parents. Actually, as it turned out to be, it was by no means as simple and easy as that!

The crew, wearing their traditional red stocking caps—although the coxswain had a peaked cap—blue jerseys and cork lifebelts, clambered on board.

Many willing hands—for quite a crowd of villagers and visitors had collected—urged the lifeboat down the inclined slipway. Her engines were pulsating well before she entered her native

element. Within twenty minutes of the firing of
the warning signal the lifeboat was afloat and
speeding to the rescue.

But what was happening to the two boys, one
aged nine and the other five, somewhere out there
in that confused turmoil of vicious sea?

When a few days ago, while the lifeboat had
not been available, a youth had been stranded on
Black Rock, the local police had appealed to
Bernard and Phil for their assistance by means of
their helicopter.

The present situation was different. The lifeboat, recently returned to her station after overhaul, was the recognized and certainly the best
means of attempting the rescue of the two missing
children.

Inside the lifeboat house one of the officials
was keeping in direct touch with the coxswain by
means of wireless telephony. At frequent intervals the receiver at the shore end transmitted the
rescuer's reports to the now considerable crowd.

An hour passed without any definite news.

Then Charlie Bickerton, only a quarter of an
hour beyond the time fixed for his meeting with
the chums, arrived at the rendezvous. Like them,
he'd put all thoughts of the question of the report
in the *Evening Monitor* out of his head. Something—red-hot news—was under way. He hadn't
long been a reporter, but what he missed from lack
of experience he made up for by his enthusiasm
for his profession.

He was busy with note-book and pencil when the voice of the R.N.L.I. official boomed over a loudspeaker.

" The cox'n reports that the rubber dinghy has been found, half full of water. There are no signs of its two former occupants. The lifeboat is encountering patches of mist, sometimes limiting visibility to less than a hundred yards."

The crowd outside the boathouse heard this announcement in almost complete silence. Many of them could draw an accurate mental picture of the scene. Almost all seemed to sense the chances of a rescue were becoming more and more doubtful. The fact that the dinghy had been found, half full of water, seemed to confirm the crowd's misgivings.

Five minutes later it was announced that the lifeboat had abandoned her search down wind— the children would have been drowned by now had they been tipped out of the dinghy into the sea—and that search would be made in the vicinity of the East Ling Bank.

Fishermen and other seafaring folk in the crowd shook their heads. They knew the East Ling Bank—a patch of hard sand intersected by deep gullies and covered at a quarter flood tide. At this very moment the highest part would be submerged.

Nevertheless the lifeboat tore off at full speed. She was still more than two hundred yards from the edge of the shoal when the bowman shouted that there was someone with head and shoulders visible above the surface.

Only one?

No, there were two—one of the missing children immersed almost to his chin was supporting his younger brother.

Then came a set-back.

With a crunching sound the lifeboat's forefoot struck the sandy bottom. She continued to scrape along for about three times her own length, only to be brought to a standstill.

An expanse of agitated water—roughly two hundred yards—separated the grounded lifeboat from its immediate objective, the two small boys in imminent danger of being covered by the rising tide.

Something had to be done and that quickly.

The resourcefulness of the lifeboatmen rose to the occasion.

Taking the end of a lifeline with them, the bowman and the second mechanic jumped overboard. Alternately wading and swimming—for there were several deep gullies to be crossed—they battled their way to the spot where the two children were, with the elder one still holding his small brother, who was already out of his depth.

Then both men, each carrying one of the boys on his back, began their struggle through the still rapidly rising tideway back to the lifeboat.

All that while, since the wireless telephonic

message that the children had been sighted, no news had been sent to the shore station. The lifeboatmen's attention was too fully occupied in other directions.

Then, after a seemingly interminable period of suspense, the great news came through.

The two missing children had been snatched from the jaws of death and were safe, though greatly exhausted, on board the lifeboat.

" There must have been an enormous strain on that lifeline," remarked Bernard to his chum.

" Yes," agreed Phil. " I wonder if it is a local product."

" No,' tain't," declared a man in the crowd who had overheard their words. " 'Twur made in Bridport, that wur."

Without further explanation he moved away, without giving the chums a chance to question him on the matter.

" Apparently he's not a Brinkwater man," observed Phil. " He's evidently interested in rope-making, and from the tone of his voice he doesn't think much of Tankerton's output."

Bernard and Philip did not wait for the life-boat's return. Nor did they attempt to get in touch with Bickerton about the report in the *Evening Monitor*. That would be, as Phil put it, a pleasure in store! In any case, the reporter was too fully occupied with his preliminary notes on the rescue, although his strenuous time was still to come when he interviewed the coxswain and crew of the lifeboat.

" I'm jolly hungry," admitted Bernard as they reached the front gate of Sea View. " Dashed if I know why, because I put away an enor-mous lunch. It must be one of the effects of the salt air."

" I vote we don't look at Bickerton's rag until after tea," suggested Phil.

" There's baked pilchards—a proper Dorset dish," announced their landlady, when they were inside the house. " And there'll be a couple of letters for you. They came by this afternoon's post."

" Thank you, Mrs. Marshbarrow," said both chums politely.

" I've put them on the mantelpiece," she con-

tinued. " And now I'll bring you in your teas.
Pilchards are best eaten piping hot!"

As soon as the landlady had gone out of the
room Bernard removed the two envelopes and
with an expressive grunt handed one to his
companion.

Both knew who had written them. They were
addressed in the same handwriting. Except for
the Hawkscar post-mark there was nothing to
indicate their origin. They weren't addressed
either to Sub-Inspector Bradfield or to Sub-
Inspector Preston; only plain " Mister " in both
cases. Nor was there the usual " On His Majesty's
Service " with the words " Royal Air Constabulary: North-eastern Division " printed on the
backs of the envelopes.

Yet, without these clues, the chums had no
doubt as to the sender's identity.

Chief Inspector Standish had written to them
—but about what? Probably it was a severe
" ticking off " over the paucity of their recent
report and over their failure to obtain satisfactory
results from their investigations.

The letters were on almost identical lines. In
them Standish made no adverse reference to their
apparent lack of success. He pointed out that,
according to reports, no act of sabotage had
occurred at Brinkwater Rope Walk since their
arrival. Therefore, their presence was of the
nature of a deterrent.

But, Standish continued, they were there to

solve a mystery and to effect an arrest—or possibly more than one. How long they were to remain at Brinkwater depended partly upon the Chief Constable of Dorset's decision as to the limit of their stay. The costs of that were being borne by that county, Bradfield and Preston being "loaned" from the North-eastern Division of the Air Constabulary.

"Standish is awfully decent about it all," remarked Phil. "I suppose he's right when he says we're curbing the saboteur's activities. That fire the other night wasn't due to saboteurs. Tankerton was certain on that point."

They discussed the matter over their meal, the pilchards growing almost stone cold during the process.

"It seems to me that if we are to nab anyone, we'd better clear right out of here," suggested Phil.

Bernard raised his eyebrows in surprise.

"Just what do you mean?" he asked.

His chum told him.

"It's worth trying," declared Bernard. "There won't be much harm done if it doesn't come off. There's a fifty-fifty chance that it will."

After further discussion they turned their attention to another matter—Charlie Bickerton's report in the *Evening Monitor* on the rescue of the boy from Black Rock.

Taking the paper from his pocket, Bernard found the article. Actually it didn't require much finding. The headlines were splashed across the front page:

GALLANT RESCUE BY TWO AIRMEN VISITORS TO BRINKWATER

Bernard read the story aloud. It was quite a good effort on Bickerton's part. Obviously he had the makings of a successful journalist, although some of his descriptive work was of rather a hectic nature.

It was the concluding paragraph that raised the chums' ire:

" The names of the two brilliant young airmen who effected the rescue are Bernard Bradfield and Philip Preston, whose homes are at Hawkscar, a village in the North Riding of Yorkshire, and who, in their helicopter known simply as H.104, are on holiday in the West Country with their headquarters at Brinkwater."

" Just wait till I get hold of that ass Bickerton!" exclaimed Bernard.

" And me too!" added his chum, expressively though ungrammatically.

An hour later—they were still discussing the offending newspaper report—they caught sight of a motor cyclist dismounting and preparing to wheel his mount up the front garden path.

It was Bickerton.

The chums went to the door to let him in. They didn't want Mrs. Marshbarrow and perhaps Jasper Nightingale to be hovering within earshot.

The reporter began his explanations without any preamble.

" I've only just finished phoning my copy about the lifeboat rescue," he announced. " Frightful swot, but my editor is frightfully bucked over it. Then I remembered I'd promised to meet you at the lifeboat house this afternoon. I saw you both and you saw me; but I ask you: how could we have a chin-wag with all that shemozzle going on? So the next best thing I could do was to pop along and see you as soon as I'd got my report off. And here I am. You've read about your rescue of the boy stranded on Black Rock in the paper I left with you? Jolly good piece of journalism, isn't it?"

He paused for breath and was on the point of continuing his pæan of self-praise when Bernard chipped in:

" That report of yours was all right up to a certain point, but why for goodness' sake did you spill the beans by letting out that we belong to the Air Constabulary?"

" I didn't!" declared Bickerton emphatically. " I took jolly good care to mention that you were holidaying here."

" You certainly did," agreed Bradfield, " but you also mentioned that we were from the Yorkshire village of Hawkscar. Well, there isn't a village at Hawkscar. It's the main depot of the North-eastern Division of the Royal Air Constabulary, as most crooks engaged in smuggling, sabotage and the like know to their cost. And is

it at all likely that two civilians should be holidaying here with a helicopter of Air Constabulary
type even though its official markings have been
painted out? You might just as well have gone
the whole hog and stated that we were sub-
inspectors of the Air Constabulary engaged to
track down suspected saboteurs at the Brinkwater
Rope Walk."

"I am sorry—I am really," declared Bickerton.
"If I'd only thought—I'd give almost anything
to put things straight."

"'What's done cannot be undone,'" quoted
Phil, joining in the discussion for the first time.

"What price a tied-up parcel?" countered the
reporter with a cheerful grin.

"Well, you know what is meant," continued
Bernard. "You said you were sorry, so that puts
paid to our complaint. You've offered to do
almost everything to straighten things out. Now's
your chance!"

"How?" asked Bickerton.

"In future are you willing to refrain from
sending in any reports concerning our activities
until either Preston or I have read them?"

"A sort of press censorship?"

"Something like it," conceded Bernard. "And
we, on our part, will keep you informed of any
future developments and see that you'll be present
if there's any likelihood of an arrest being made."

The reporter extended a thin, ink-stained hand.

"That's a deal," he declared. "But is there

any chance of your making an arrest in the near future?"

"Not one, as far as we know," replied Bernard. "But we live in hopes."

"We're clearing out of here to-morrow," announced Phil.

"What! leaving for good?" asked the reporter.

"Oh no! we'll be back not later than Saturday. We think of paying a visit to Bere Regis Aerodrome to see our mutual friend, Williamson."

"He was no friend of mine," declared Bickerton. "He got me fired all right. But I don't bear him any malice. Give him my kind regards when you see him."

The chums promised that they would, even though they were none too sure of the nature of their reception by their former employer.

Then, after a few more minutes' conversation, Bickerton took his leave.

"There's just time to catch Tankerton before supper," observed Phil, as soon as the noise of the reporter's motor cycle had been lost in the distance. "We ought to inform him that we're going away for a few days."

"Rather!" agreed his friend. "It would never do to clear out without letting him know!"

The manager of the Brinkwater Rope Walk was not at home. The chums then made their way to the next likely place—the Crab and Lobster. They found Tankerton about to finish a game of billiards. He was the winner. He had

had more than one glass of ale. Consequently he was in high spirits.

"Good evening, you fellows!" he exclaimed boisterously. "Read Bickerton's tripe yet? But of course I'd forgotten I'd promised to send someone along with a copy. 'Visitors from Yorkshire' indeed! I must say that's a good one!"

"We've already seen the paper," said Phil.

The chums could not help feeling annoyed at Tankerton's outburst, particularly as there were strangers present.

"Bickerton's admitted his mistake," added Bernard. "He also apologized, so there's nothing more to be done about *that*. But we'd like a word with you in private, if you don't mind."

"I mind? Man, I'm on top of the world," asserted Tankerton, struggling into his coat. "To-day I've been given a couple of big Government contracts, one for Devonport and the other for Portsmouth dockyards. That'll keep me busy for a bit."

"I hope it will," said Phil politely.

The manager raised his eyebrows.

"I don't quite get you," he protested. "I always am busy."

"There's no need for you to be huffy," rejoined Phil. "You seem to have taken what I said in the wrong way. Probably I didn't express myself very well."

"That's all right," declared Tankerton, his face now wreathed in smiles. "But it has been a busy time in the works. That fire didn't ease matters. The fire insurance representative came down and passed our claim, and already the damaged foot-bridge has been repaired—but I suppose you know that already."

"We didn't," replied Bernard. "We haven't used the right-of-way through the rope-walk since the fire."

"Has Nightingale?" asked the manager.

"I don't think so," answered Bernard. "He's down with a heavy cold. He hasn't been out of the house for several days—at least, I don't think he has."

By this time the chums had succeeded in shepherding the slightly bemused Tankerton beyond the precincts of the Crab and Lobster.

"We've been chasing you to tell you we're going away for a day or so," announced Phil.

Evidently the latter part of this statement didn't register in the manager's mind. It was the first four words that caused him resentment.

"Chasing me, have you?" he protested. "Let me tell you straight that outside of business hours I'm my own master and not answerable to Sir Montague Corton——"

"We needn't go into that now," interrupted Bernard. "We hadn't a chance to tell you earlier. It's this—we're going away for a day or so."

"Are you?" rejoined Tankerton with a quick show of interest. "When will you be back?"

" Not later than Saturday. We're paying a visit to some of our former colleagues at Bere Regis."

" Do you expect to find any clues to what's been going on here in the sabotage line?" asked the manager.

" Absolutely none," declared Bernard. " I don't suppose we'll mention that subject while we're there."

" And supposing there's another attempt at it while you're away? There hasn't been one since you arrived."

" Only Bickerton and you know of our intentions," announced Phil. " So there's precious little chance of a saboteur or saboteurs knowing where we are."

" Bickerton—that Nosey Parker," snorted the manager. " If he knows you're deserting your posts——"

" You are putting your opinion in rather an objectionable way, Mr. Tankerton," demurred Phil. " There's no question of our shirking our duty."

" Whether you are or whether you aren't doesn't affect my point," continued Tankerton. " I said—and I'll say it again—that Bickerton is a Nosey Parker; and if you've told him you're off for a few days he'll have spread the news from one end of Brinkwater to the other."

He paused as if to recover his breath. Then in a very different tone he continued:

" What have I been saying, gentlemen? Coming out of the Crab and Lobster into the fresh air must have made me lose command of my tongue. All that about deserting your posts—I take it all back. I'm sorry, I am really!"

"Then forget it," rejoined Bernard. "And now we'll be getting back and turn in early. We've quite a lot to do before we leave Brinkwater for a few days."

They walked in silence for the best part of their homeward way—if Mrs. Marshbarrow's establishment could be termed home.

"Our friend Tankerton doesn't seem to have a very good opinion of Bickerton," remarked Phil. "I wonder why?"

"Probably that's one result of looking upon the wine when it is red," quoted his chum. "But I must say that so far—so far, mind you—our little scheme is going according to plan!"

The chums turned out soon after six on the following morning to find that everything was covered by a thick mist.

" I wonder how high this lot is," asked Bernard. " We may be held up for the best part of the day."

" In a fever to get going?" rejoined his chum. " But the mist should clear well before midday. Hark! there's a jet. It can't be more than a couple of thousand feet up, if that, and it would certainly be flying above the mist. If you ask me, the fog'll clear well before noon."

They tubbed, shaved and dressed. Then they packed their urgent necessities in a couple of light cases. They were leaving most of their gear to relieve Mrs. Marshbarrow's mind—as Phil put it—from any anxiety lest they " shot the moon ".

" When shall we expect you back?" inquired their landlady, after they had had a substantial breakfast.

" Not later than Saturday," replied Phil, using precisely the same answer to a similar question asked both by Tankerton and his *bête noire*, Bickerton.

By this time the mist had entirely dispersed and the sun was shining in an unclouded sky.

There was quite a good crowd to see them off, including Mrs. Marshbarrow and all her staff and Jasper Nightingale. The village policeman was not there, so evidently he had heard nothing of the impending helicopter ascent.

In the adjacent grounds of Peacehaven—where H.104 had been garaged in the open—Mrs. Knott, the proprietress, was waiting with her quota of visitors plus most of her domestic and outdoor staff.

" One would think we were starting on a flight round the world," said Bernard to his chum. " All it wants is a brass band and a loudspeaker to advertise the fact!"

They clambered on board, Bradfield taking the pilot's seat.

He pressed the starter.

Nothing happened.

The electrical system seemed to be as dead as mutton.

He made a second attempt with similar results.

They had run the engine on the previous day, and it had functioned perfectly. Now Bernard couldn't get a kick out of it.

" The mist has affected the plugs, I guess," suggested Phil. " I'll have them out and test them."

He lifted the cowling and removed the plugs. There appeared to be nothing wrong with them.

There was no sign of damp and the spark gaps were at the correct setting. He traced the leads back to the distributor. There was nothing wrong there.

Then he ran his finger along the switch wire under the dash.

There the fault lay. The insulated wire was adrift. Quite probably the connection had been loosened by excessive vibration, but on H.104 there was very little vibration.

Phil pulled the wire clear. It came quite freely.

He gave an exclamation of annoyance—alarm, perhaps—that made his chum inquire what was up.

" Dirty work here, old son," announced Phil in a low voice, so that none of the crowd could hear. " The wire's been cut!"

There could be but very little doubt about that. The insulated wire had most decidedly been severed, presumably by a pair of cutters.

It might have been another instance of sabotage. As in the numerous cases in connection with the maliciously damaged ropes, it entailed no immediate danger to anyone. The helicopter couldn't possibly take off until the damage had been made good. If, on the other hand, the engine had " packed up " while in flight, it might very well have resulted in loss of life or limb.

The lead was joined up again in a little less than five minutes. The engine then fired at the first touch of the starter push.

" Everything's O.K. now, I think," said Phil, still speaking in a low voice, so as not to be overheard by any of the onlookers. " We may as well be getting along."

It was—or it ought to be—at most a thirty minutes' run from Brinkwater to Bere Regis. The helicopter rose almost vertically to a height of one thousand feet and then set off in the required direction. Both pilots knew this part of the country so well that they had no occasion to use their map.

They were a little to the north of Dorchester when they became aware of a rasping noise coming somewhere from the mechanism—a noise that seemed to be increasing. Where the sound came from they could not at once determine. It might be due to the main bearing becoming overheated or it might be something in connection with the helices.

Even so there was very little danger to be apprehended unless excessive friction caused fire to break out. The ignition could be switched off and the helicopter would made a retarded drop to earth, the rate of its descent checked by the horizontal blades.

" Coming down?" bawled Phil.

" No; we're nearly there," replied his chum. " I can nurse her that distance, I think."

Throttling back the engine, Bernard began to put his intentions into practice.

The noise continued, but without any notice-

able increase in volume, until Bere Regis Aerodrome came in sight.

Then something did happen. From the top of
the shaft around which the helices were turning a
thin column of brownish smoke appeared. That
meant trouble. Evidently the lubricating system
had developed a fault and the resulting friction
was on the point of starting a fire. If that
happened, its seat would be somewhere where
a fire extinguisher would be of little or no use.

Having heard Bernard's decision, Phil sat
quietly in his bucket seat. He had complete
confidence in his chum to do the right thing.

Forty-five seconds later, the pilot switched off
the ignition. More smoke was issuing from the
column. At any moment flames would appear
and the helices would seize-up.

With the following wind, Bernard calculated
that the now slowly falling helicopter would touch
down somewhere within the perimeter of the
aerodrome. If humanly possible he must avoid
alighting upon one of the hangars or upon the
roofs of the machine-shops or the office buildings,
or, what was even more important, upon one of
the numerous aircraft dotted about what were once
the runways.

Bere Regis Aerodrome had once been a ter-
minus for long-distance aircraft. Improvements
in size and design, with a corresponding increase
of horse-power, had rendered the runways
obsolete. When the present company took over,

the use of the drome had been restricted to helicopters, their range of operation being limited to the confines of the British Isles.

As H.104 began her inclined and involuntary descent her crew could see that there were between twenty and thirty helicopters of various types, dispersed more or less regularly in rectangles marked in white paint.

It was touch and go, but somehow Bernard contrived to land his helicopter in a vacant place within a couple of feet of the next aircraft.

Feeling a little shaken—the impact had blown one of the tyres—the chums scrambled out. Three or four of the ground staff came running up.

" Hey, what do you think you're doing?" demanded the charge-hand of the party. " What do you mean barging in like that and never giving any signal that you were——"

He broke off abruptly. His eyes opened wide and a cheerful grin appeared upon his face.

" Why if it ain't Mr. Bradfield! And Mr. Preston too. I never expected to see you here again."

" We hoped we'd see you, Lane," rejoined Bernard diplomatically. " We wondered if you were still here."

" I am, and likely to be a goodish while," said the charge-hand. " You're still in the air police, I see."

" We are," admitted Phil. " Even though we're in mufti. But how did you know that?"

"I wouldn't be much good at my job if I couldn't recognize an air police helicopter even if her distinctive marks are painted out," declared Lane. "It was lucky for you to be able to make here with a conked-out engine."

"We intended coming here in any case," declared Phil. "Just to see some of our former colleagues. Is Mr. Williamson anywhere about?"

"He'll be in his office, I reckon," replied Lane. "You'll be wanting some repairs? Directly the boss lets me know I'll be getting on with the job. Priority work for former members of the staff, you know," he added with an expressive wink.

The chums made their way in the direction of the branch manager's office. They passed quite a number of pilots and mechanics, all with unfamiliar faces. Apparently Williamson was fond of changes in his staff.

They were shown into his private room.

"Bless my soul, this is a surprise!" exclaimed Williamson. "Still in the air police? You're not in uniform, I see."

It was almost the same question that had been put to them by Charge-hand Lane.

"Still in it," replied Bernard.

"Well, jolly good luck to you," was the effusive rejoinder.

"We'll need it," declared Phil.

"Oh! how's that?" asked Williamson. "Anything I can do? I take it that that's why you're here. But before we go any further let me explain—apologize even—the reason why I had to ask you to resign from the company's service, Bradfield. You knew that it was against orders for any of our helicopters to fly anywhere outside the British Isles. You crashed your machine within a few miles of the Belgian coast."

"I hadn't the slightest intention of flying out of the country when I took off," announced Bernard. "But when a fellow has the muzzle of an automatic stuck into his ribs, that's a pretty one-sided argument, I fancy."

"It certainly is," agreed Williamson. "But, of course, I knew nothing of the circumstances at the time. When I did it was too late. You, Bradfield, had been given your discharge and you, Preston, I take it, had sent me your resignation out of loyalty to your brother pilot. I am sorry, but on the other hand it afforded you the opportunity to improve your prospects by joining the Air Constabulary."

"That's quite all right," declared Bernard, speaking on behalf of his chum as well as for himself. "But we haven't come to see you about that."

"Then what?" prompted the manager.

"We were making for here from Brinkwater when we developed engine trouble—what exactly it was we don't know."

"We soon will," promised Williamson. "I'll get a couple of our mechanics on the job straight away. A priority job, you understand. But, excuse my asking, who pays? You, or does it come out of the police funds?"

"The police, I hope," replied Phil.

The possibility of the chums having to pay for the repairs hadn't occurred to him. A lot depended upon the successful or unsuccessful sequel to their visit to Bere Regis Aerodrome.

"Apart from your slight mishap, what brings you here to see me?" prompted Williamson. "Of course, if you wish it I'll keep the matter entirely to myself."

Thus encouraged, Bernard, prompted occasionally by his chum, began to sketch the circumstances under which they had been sent south to Brinkwater.

"Wait a moment!" interrupted Williamson, in the course of the narrative. "This is interesting! You say that a saboteur has been tampering with the Brinkwater Rope Walk's output. Back last May we gave them an order for a dozen tow-ropes. You know the sort: made of three-inch manilla with an eye at each end. Two of them parted when they were first used. We sent the rest back, pointing out that the defects might have caused a serious accident. If that was a case of sabotage one cannot blame the makers of the stuff. So if I can help to lay the culprits by the heels, just let me know if there's anything I can do. But fire away!"

Without further interruptions Bernard completed his account of what had happened at Brinkwater to date.

"And we told quite a number of people that we were going to Bere Regis and that we'd be away till Saturday," said Bernard.

"No, we didn't," contradicted his companion. "What we took good care to say was that we'd be back *not later than* Saturday."

"My error!" exclaimed Bernard cheerfully.

"What was the idea?" asked Williamson.

"To give the saboteur, if he was anywhere about, the chance of having another go while we're away," explained Bernard. "We propose flying back to Brinkwater shortly before midnight——"

"In your bus?" interrupted the manager. "Dash it all, Bradfield! We pride ourselves upon the speed and efficiency of our repair services, but from what we've already heard I very much doubt whether your helicopter will be air-worthy before Friday."

"We had no intention of flying our bus back to-night," announced Bernard. "We meant to ask you if you would let us have one of your helicopters, complete with pilot, and get him to land us in a secluded meadow about half a mile from Brinkwater."

"I'll arrange for that to be done," agreed Williamson, without any hesitation. "At what time do you propose to start?"

"At twenty-three-o-o," replied Bernard. "If

he can drop us at about ten minutes to twelve that should give us an ample margin of time."

They continued to discuss the arrangements.

" You'll want some sleep," remarked Williamson.

" We'll be fresh enough without," declared Phil, somewhat boastfully. " We're used to long hours at our job."

" But it may keep you up all night and well into the next day," the manager pointed out. " If you take my advice you'll turn in after lunch and sleep until just before dinner. You'll regard yourselves as my guests, of course."

His two former pilots thanked him. This was a very different Williamson from the man they had known during their initial training at Bere Regis Aerodrome.

" By the by, I've a message for you," said Phil. " Charles Bickerton wishes to be remembered to you."

" Bickerton? Where did you run across him?"

" He's a reporter on the staff of the Dorset *Evening Monitor*. He told us he was a pilot here. That was after we left."

A grim smile appeared on the manager's face.

" Then it is to be hoped that he'll make a better reporter than he did a pilot," he rejoined. " And now you'd better see your man."

He touched a bell, and then took a large-scale map and laid it out on a table.

" Send Mr. Carrick to me, please!" he ordered when a messenger arrived.

In a few minutes Carrick appeared. He was the pilot who was to take Bradfield and Preston back to Brinkwater; a big, broad-shouldered man of about twenty-five who looked more like a professional boxer than an airman.

Briefly, and at Williamson's invitation, Bernard and Phil outlined the plan of campaign. Carrick was to drop them inside square C.9, as shown on the map. This was in a meadow a hundred yards north of the Brinkwater-Dorchester road, and less than a mile from the Brinkwater Rope Walk. Carrick would then return to Bere Regis without delay.

These preliminaries settled, the two chums joined the staff at lunch. After that they made more or less a pretence at sleeping until seven, when dinner was served. Whatever changes had taken place at Bere Regis Aerodrome since the chums had been pilots there, it was very evident that the standard of meals had improved tremendously!

" A phone message came through at six o'clock from the Brinkwater police," announced Williamson, at the conclusion of the meal.

" For us?" asked Bernard in a tone of mild surprise.

" No; not exactly. They asked if H.104 had landed here. The operator replied that it had."

" What's the bright idea?" asked Phil. " As

far as we know, Constable Jenkins was unaware of our leaving Brinkwater. Do you mind, sir, if we phone through and ask him the reason?"

" Not in the least," replied Williamson. " You can use the extension in my office."

Phil got through to the policeman's cottage without much difficulty. Jenkins was at home and he answered the call.

" What's the bright idea, Jenkins?" asked Phil, after he'd given his name.

" What idea, sir?"

" Ringing up to know whether H.104 was here."

" I never rung up, sir," declared the constable emphatically. " Where are you calling from? From Bere Regis Aerodrome, sir? Bless me! Until you told me I'd no idea that your machine was anywhere but parked in Mrs. Knott's back garden at Brinkwater!"

" That call came from the fellow we're after," suggested Phil after he had rung off. " It's a try-on to discover whether or not we're at Bere Regis. I think I can hazard a couple of guesses who the fellow is. Bernard, my festive, something's going to happen to-night, or rather in the small hours of to-morrow. I feel it in my bones!"

" Let's hope to goodness you're right," rejoined his chum.

Accompanied by the drome manager, who seldom appeared to witness the departure of his clients, but now seemed to be keenly interested in the affairs of the Brinkwater Rope Walk, Bernard and Phil made their way to the " pitch " —there seemed no other description of it—where Pilot Carrick was waiting to transport them to what they hoped would be the scene of operations.

On the way they passed the square upon which H.104 had awkwardly alighted. Their machine was no longer there. The staff had wasted no time in moving the damaged helicopter to the repair shop and getting on with the job.

Dead on time the chums arrived at the arranged spot. Carrick and two groundmen were standing by. The engine had been set in motion and the helices were " idling " as they turned slowly and silently in the semi-darkness of the night.

The helicopter was a four-seater and consequently larger than the standard types used by the Royal Air Constabulary. It was no stranger to Bernard and Phil, who had frequently flown machines of identically the same pattern until they had severed their connection with the Inter-British Airways Company.

Pilot and passengers clambered on board.

With a gradual increase of throttle the helicopter began to quiver. Then, almost imperceptibly, it parted company with Mother Earth and climbed vertically into space.

Bernard could not help experiencing a slight feeling of apprehension once they were airborne. It was akin to that almost unaccountable sensation of mistrust that many car drivers feel when they are in another man's car, and they are imagining that he's doing the wrong thing.

He would not have experienced that sensation had Phil been at the controls. A sense of harmony existed between the pair. Each of them thought the other could do no wrong, or rather, if one of them was under the impression that the other wasn't doing the right thing or was taking needless risks, he still felt complete confidence in him.

So Bernard sat back in his bucket-seat, crossed his fingers and hoped for the best.

On the other hand, Phil felt no such qualms. He, too, sat back, quivering with excitement at the prospect of possible action. Quite a lot of signs pointed to that, particularly the telephone call, purporting to come from the Brinkwater police but which was evidently made to reassure the mysterious sender that the two Air Constabulary officers were nicely out of the way, leaving the coast clear for him to pursue his highly illegal activities.

It was a fairly dark, cloudless night. Only a

few stars were visible, yet in spite of the paucity
of light, objects some two thousand feet below
could be readily identified.

Arriving over his immediate destination Carrick
had some difficulty in locating it—a field bounded
on all sides by a tall hedge, with a derelict stall
or stable at the south-western corner. Three
times he circled around until Bernard gave him
its position.

The rest seemed easy.

The pilot brought the helicopter to ground.
The chums alighted, each hampered by the suit-
case he was carrying. Having previously surveyed
the field, they had decided to hide their impedimenta under the rafters of the shed and to recover
them at the earliest opportunity.

They were on the point of thanking their pilot
when they heard the sounds of a decidedly noisy
car approaching along the nearby road, which was
separated from their temporary parking ground
by another and slightly larger field.

There were two cars. One stopped to the
accompaniment of grinding brakes. The other
carried on for a short distance. Then it, too, came
to an abrupt and noisy standstill.

" Confound them!" ejaculated Phil. " What's
the idea, pulling up here in the dead of night?"

" Poachers, perhaps," suggested his chum.
" Do you mind switching off?" he continued,
addressing the pilot.

Carrick did so. The car engines, too, were

silent, although the slamming of doors pointed to the fact that the occupants were alighting.

For what purpose? Bernard's surmise might prove to be a correct one. There had been several instances of poaching on a large scale in the county by gangs operating with cars. It could be profitable, with wild rabbits fetching six shillings each in the shops.

Leaving Carrick seated in the helicopter, the chums went to the hedge. Peering over the top, they saw a somewhat startling sight.

There were about a dozen men coming across the adjoining field. Four were making straight for it; the others, split into two groups, were advancing to right and left with the evident intention of throwing a cordon around it.

They were uniformed men. Some were wearing Dorset Constabulary headgear, others were members of the Customs and Excise.

The chums retreated to the now silent helicopter.

An inspector, followed by three constables, climbed the stile in the hedge and approached them.

" I'm a police officer!" announced the inspector. " You are under arrest. I must warn you that any statement you might make may be used in evidence——"

" Sorry to disillusion you, Inspector!" interrupted Bernard. " But it happens that we—at least two of us—are also police officers."

Even in the faint starlight it was possible to

see the look of mingled suspicion, surprise and disappointment on the inspector's face.

" Might I see your warrant cards?" he asked.

By this time the rest of the party had arrived upon the scene. Perhaps they, too, were disappointed by not being ordered to " clap the darbies " on the three suspects.

The inspector flashed a torchlight upon the proffered documents.

" So you are the two Air Constabulary officers loaned to us for special duty," he observed. " Of course we know all about you. It looks as if we're at cross purposes."

" Obviously a mistake somewhere," added Bernard.

Briefly the inspector explained the situation from his point of view. Information had been received that a vessel had been lying off the coast and that a valuable consignment of contraband goods was to be taken off her during the night by helicopter.

The police and customs men had spotted the Bere Regis machine as it circled to find its temporary landing-ground, and since that spot was in a remote region, they had jumped to the erroneous conclusion that this was their quarry.

Then equally briefly Bradfield told the inspector the reason that brought the helicopter there at that time of night.

" I hope we haven't queered your pitch," observed the latter.

"If you can avoid going near Brinkwater on your way back, I don't think you'll upset our plans," rejoined Bernard.

This the inspector promised to do.

"Except that one of my men is stationed there," he added.

That gave Bernard an idea.

"I suppose you don't know anything of a telephone call to Bere Regis Aerodrome this evening purporting to come from the police and inquiring if our helicopter—not this one—was there?"

"Certainly not," declared the inspector emphatically. "If it had been put through at Bridport I should have known it. I hadn't the faintest idea that you had gone to Bere Regis. I'll ask the local constable if he knows anything about it. He's here now—Constable Jenkins!"

"Sir?" answered that worthy.

"I've already phoned this constable, Inspector," announced Phil.

"That's no reason why he shouldn't be asked again," declared Jenkins's superior officer; then addressing the Brinkwater policeman:

"Constable Jenkins, did you phone through to Bere Regis Aerodrome to ask if H.104 had landed there?"

"No, sir; I did not. I was off duty and at home from two till eight, when I reported for duty according to your instructions. During that time I phoned twice—I've recorded them in the

log-book, sir—and received three calls. In none
of them was Bere Regis or H.104 mentioned."

"That seems good enough," remarked the
inspector, motioning Jenkins to rejoin the rest of
the party, who were standing a slight distance
away.

"Do you mind if I say something to Constable
Jenkins, Inspector?" asked Phil.

"Not in the least."

"We want you, constable, not to mention the
fact to anybody that you saw Sub-Inspector
Bradfield and myself here to-night," said Phil.
"We're not here for the good of our healths but
with a definite object in view. One careless
sentence might wreck all our plans."

"That's all right, sir," declared Jenkins. "The
only person I'm likely to talk to when I come off
duty is my missus. I reckon she'll be fast asleep
in any case."

"We'd like you to keep silent about it longer
than that," continued Phil. "Don't say anything
to anyone about our being here—we're supposed
to be staying at Bere Regis—until we see you
again."

Jenkins gave the desired promise, and a few
minutes later the police and customs men withdrew, their cars chugging along the Dorchester
Road and away from Brinkwater village.

"A rum business this," commented Carrick.
"I should have thought that if the fellow or
fellows you're after did send a bogus message to

the police it would have been to lure them away from the district—not to the spot where we touched down!"

"It may be a coincidence," suggested Bernard. "There may be an attempt to smuggle contraband ashore that hasn't the faintest connection with the case we're following up."

"Then let's hope it won't muck everything up for you," rejoined the pilot as he climbed into the cockpit of his aircraft. "Well, all the best!"

Five minutes later—it was now quarter to one —the helicopter was out of sight and hearing.

"I expect we're too late," remarked Bernard dubiously.

"Yes; perhaps everything is mucked-up," added Phil.

The wave of optimism that had overrun them earlier in the evening had definitely subsided.

Having hidden their suitcases in the roof of the ramshackle shed, they set off for the rope-walk. On arriving at the eastern end of the long building they scaled the fence and with very little effort entered by means of one of the many open windows.

Then, as silently as possible, they made their way half-way along until they came to the recently repaired bridge opposite their temporary home at Sea View.

There they separated, taking up almost the same positions as those they had occupied when they had mistaken Jasper Nightingale for their man. A similar mistake was not likely to occur again, since the amateur fisherman had not properly recovered from his chill, and had not made any more nocturnal excursions.

It was dark inside the building. On the former occasion it had been moonlight. Now there was none, but in the loom of the night sky the newly "laid" ropes showed up with tolerable distinctness.

A long-drawn-out hour passed and nothing happened.

Phil came from his place of concealment to his chum's hiding-place.

"It looks as if there's nothing doing," he suggested in a low voice.

"Isn't there? Then what's that?" asked Bernard in an excited whisper.

In the far distance and in the direction of the office buildings the beam of a torchlight was playing on the ground.

As the chums watched, the faint patch of artificial light vanished. About a quarter of a minute later it reappeared. This continued until there could be no doubt about it. Someone was stealthily making his way towards them.

Then they heard footsteps, but they were not those of the person approaching by the side of the rope-walk.

A door opened. There was a dazzling beam that played almost too close to the crouching men.

A figure, carrying something like a rifle on his shoulder, mounted the steps of the footbridge.

Now the chums could see who he was. It was Nightingale carrying his disjointed rod.

Without looking either right or left he crossed the bridge. Then came the sound of a key turning in a lock, followed by the banging of a door.

Jasper Nightingale had chosen this night of all nights to resume his nocturnal fishing expeditions!

The chums heard Nightingale enter Sea View
and shut the door. They almost wished that they
could follow his example. To lie in their comfortable beds would be infinitely preferable to
keeping a vigil in a dark and decidedly chilly shed.

They waited for about another half-hour, but
all to no purpose. The suspect, whoever he might
be, had taken alarm at the sight of Nightingale's
torch. But for that they might have got their
man. Instead they were experiencing disappointment and discomfort.

Leaving the rope-walk by the same way as
they had entered it, some two hours earlier, they
trudged back to the shed where they had left their
suitcases.

They hardly spoke until they arrived at the
field where the helicopter had landed them. They
were conscious of failure. That didn't mean that
they were going to abandon their efforts; but it
did mean that they would still be unable to return
to Sea View. They would have to keep clear of
Brinkwater and to avoid all contact with it until
they had spent another night upon the scene of
operations.

They were hungry, too. Expecting to have made an arrest of the saboteur that night, they had neglected to supply themselves with anything to eat and drink.

" Botheration take that fellow Nightingale!" exclaimed Phil. " He mucked everything up. And what if he goes fishing again to-night?"

" I don't think he will," replied Bernard. " I don't remember him doing that on two nights running. Now we have to find a hide-out—somewhere where we can get food and a bed. We'll have to pitch some sort of yarn about our car having broken down!"

Soon it was broad daylight. They struck inland taking by-roads and footpaths until, having covered about six miles—heavy going since they were hampered by their suitcases—they spotted an isolated farmhouse, sheltering in a fold of the hills.

" We'll try our luck there," declared Phil.

" Don't be in such a tearing hurry," protested his companion. " It's only just gone five. There's no smoke from the chimneys. Obviously the farmer isn't up and about yet. We'll give him another three quarters of an hour."

The grass was heavy with dew, so they had to rest against the trunk of a large oak tree, making their plans of how they should approach the farmer without contradicting one another. It wouldn't take much of that to arouse his suspicions and doubts concerning his early visitors!

Presently smoke emerged from the farmhouse. Then a man appeared driving the cows into their shed for milking.

The chums waited about another quarter of an hour before knocking on the open door at the rear of the building.

A youngish, pleasant-faced woman appeared and asked, without any sign of surprise, what they wanted.

" Could we have breakfast, please?" asked Phil.

" Certainly," was the prompt response. " It'll be ready in half an hour—ham and new-laid eggs if that's to your liking. I've a couple of paying guests. I hope you won't mind having breakfast in the same room."

Soon Bernard and Phil were sitting down to an ample and hearty repast. Then the farmer came in, he, too, expressing no surprise at his early visitors and listening to the story of the broken-down car without showing any signs of doubt.

" Car's being towed into Darchester, be she?" he asked. " Well now, there's no reason why you shouldn't turn in on spare bed—there ain't no need for you to take your clothes off—and after tea I'll get you a lift in a car going to Darchester."

" It's very kind of you," said Phil, " but we can easily walk into Brinkwater and get a bus from there."

" There ain't no need for that," declared the genial and would-be helpful farmer. " We've been having a spot of bother with the County

Agricultural Committee and a reporter from the *Evening Monitor* is coming over to see me about five. He'll give you a lift back to Darchester. Charlie Bickerton—that's his name—is a right good sort. Do anyone a good turn, he will!"

" Now what's to be done?" asked Bernard, when they were alone in the room in which they hoped to make up arrears of loss of sleep. " If Bickerton gives tongue we'll look a pair of idiots. Can't we make up some excuse to get away from here well before five? That's the time the farmer's expecting him."

" We can have a shot at it," replied his chum. " But it will look decidedly fishy!"

Soon they were sound asleep. They were so tired that they slumbered on, without knowing that the midday dinner-time had come and gone, finally to be aroused by the farmer knocking on the door and announcing: " It be gone four!"

A few minutes later, still feeling drowsy, they went down to the living-room to find Bickerton already there. He had arrived an hour earlier than he'd been expected.

A look of surprise flitted over the reporter's homely features, quickly to be followed by a broad grin. But he didn't speak, waiting for the farmer to make the necessary introductions.

" These'll be the two gen'lemen I wur speaking to you about," said their host. " And this'll be Charlie Bickerton. He'll be right willin' to gi' you a lift back to Darchester."

" Of course I will," agreed the reporter. " Cars can be a problem when they pack up, can't they?"

It was now quite obvious that Bickerton was entering into the spirit of the game. He was by no means so slow in the uptake as the chums had had reason to believe.

They had tea—again a most satisfying repast —and then Bernard and Phil went for a stroll while Bickerton and the farmer discussed the action of the County Agricultural Committee. Then, just before six, the chums boarded the reporter's car.

" It's a lucky thing for us you weren't using your motor bike," observed Bernard.

" And jolly decent of you not to give us away," added Phil. " Ananias wouldn't have had a look in if you had!"

Bickerton stopped the car, only some fifty yards from the junction with a main road.

" Let's get this straight," he suggested. " You weren't on the tiles last night for nothing, I take it!"

" In confidence, of course," rejoined Phil.

He described in a fairly comprehensive manner the events leading up to and including their fruit- less vigil, ending with the chums' resolve to spend another night in the rope-works.

" And how are you putting in your time before midnight?" asked Bickerton.

" Hanging on the slack, as we did yesterday, I suppose."

" You won't!" declared the reporter emphatic-

10

ally. " I'm driving you to Dorchester. We can have supper there. I have to see my editor, but that won't take long. Then I'll drive you back to wherever you wish near Brinkwater at any time you wish."

" I say, that's asking too much of you," protested Bernard.

" Not at all," rejoined Bickerton. " I've a flower show to do there to-morrow, so I'll put up at the Crab and Lobster."

" All the same, it's jolly decent of you," reiterated Bernard.

" But I'm not doing it for nothing," continued the reporter with another of his expansive smiles. " I want you to keep me informed of what's happening—I've already given you my word not to mention the matter in my paper until you agree—and when the story can come out you'll give me six hours' start over the other county newspapers?"

" Right!" exclaimed Bernard, and Phil nodded in agreement.

" Good enough!" declared Bickerton. " And we won't want to see a lawyer about that."

The chums spent quite a pleasant though restful evening in the reporter's digs, and it was not until a quarter to eleven that they set off towards Brinkwater in Bickerton's car.

" Won't you be too late to get into the Crab and Lobster?" asked Bernard.

" No jolly fear!" replied the pressman exuberantly. " I've booked a room and the landlord will let me in at any hour of the day or night. But I'll tell you what: I'll come along with you, if you like, and keep watch for the fellow. I may be useful if it comes to a scrap. I'm still pretty handy with my fists, and, of course, my promise not to say or write anything till you give me leave still holds."

Bernard hardly knew what to say. He couldn't consult his chum, who was occupying the rear seat, without the driver overhearing the conversation.

" What will you do with your car?" he asked.

" Easy! I'll put you two down, drive to the pub, garage the old bus and walk back to you."

" But that won't work," objected Bradfield. " The saboteur, if he's anywhere about, might spot you coming away from the village. That's something we have to guard against."

" I suppose so," admitted Bickerton in a crest-fallen tone. " But look here: what's to prevent me from parking the old bus by the side of the road? Then we can all sit pretty until it's time to take up positions."

" And during the night someone pinches the car—what then?"

" They won't—they just can't," declared Bickerton. " I've a little gadget here—it's so cute that I'm thinking of patenting it—that's absolutely—absolutely, I repeat—foolproof and all that. I'll show you."

They were now about six miles from Brink-

water.   Bickerton stopped the car and switched
off the headlights.

" Too many drivers put their trust in a switch
concealed under the dash," he continued.   " Car
thieves are wise to that.   Now see that dial?   It
looks like an oil-indicator, doesn't it?"

He pointed to one of the instruments on the
illuminated dashboard.   It looked something like
an aneroid barometer, with a centrally pivoted
hand and numbered nought to twenty round the
edge of the face.

" It points to fifteen—that's the secret number,"
Bickerton went on.   " Now I'll alter the hand to
any other number you like.   I press the starter
—nothing happens.   The engine is as dead as
Julius Cæsar's aunt.   Nothing will induce it to
fire until I've put the indicator back to fifteen.
That's my concealed switch.   It would take a
Number One Smart Aleck to find that."

His passengers agreed that it appeared to be a
most ingenious device.

Bickerton put the needle back till it registered
fifteen.   Then he switched on the ignition and
pressed the starter.

Except for the whirring of the flywheel nothing
happened.

He made a second attempt with similar results.

" I've never known that to happen before,"
declared the somewhat crestfallen owner.   " It
can't be the switch.   I wonder if there's a break
in one of the wires."

He fiddled with every switch on the dashboard.

He turned on the headlamps and turned them off again, repeating the operation several times in the vain hope that by so doing the ignition would again function.

" Must have a look under the bonnet," he declared. " Will you switch on, old man, when I sing out?"

He got out of the car, raised the bonnet and flashed a torch on to the silent engine.

It was then that Phil heard the sound of an approaching aircraft. In ordinary circumstances there was nothing unusual about that; but this was different. It was a helicopter hovering around at quite a low altitude, probably looking for somewhere to touch down—or was it? Was its approach the result of curiosity on its pilot's part? Had he any reason to investigate the meaning of those intermittent lights coming from the stationary car?

" Give him the O.K., Bickerton!" exclaimed Bernard.

He wouldn't have been at all surprised if the owner of the car had asked why. But Bickerton rose to the occasion. Holding his torch skywards, he flashed two letters in morse.

The helicopter was now only about one hundred feet up. It was hovering and making no attempt to descend. A rather significant thing about it was that it was showing no navigation lights—nor lights of any description. There it hung, apparently motionless yet sharply defined against the starlit sky.

Then a dark elongated object dropped from it, falling rapidly until it was about thirty feet from the ground. A parachute opened in order to check the rate of its descent, but even so it hit the road with a thud. Five yards nearer it would have struck the car, with serious consequences to the occupants.

The heavy package had hardly struck the road when another and similar one followed. This came down comparatively slowly to land on a hedge by the side of the road.

" Give him another O.K.!" whispered Bernard.

By now he was firmly convinced that this was the attempt to be made to land contraband from a vessel somewhere out in the English Channel. The police inspector had marshalled some of his facts correctly, but he had set his trap twenty-four hours too soon!

Again Bickerton complied without demur.

For a minute or so there was no response from the crew of the smugglers' aircraft. Were they expecting the O.K. in a different, prearranged code?

Evidently not, for to the relief of the three on the ground, the helicopter increased speed and in a couple of minutes was out of sight as it made off in a southerly direction towards the coast.

" This is your do, old man!" declared Bernard.

" What do you mean?" asked Bickerton.

" The smugglers—whoever they are—have presented you with a couple of bags of contraband," explained Bradfield. " What the reward will be, I don't know. It depends upon what the stuff consists of."

" But you two are in it too," declared the reporter.

" We've quite enough on our hands at the moment," said Bernard. " It's just by chance we happen to be here. We'll give you a hand to place these bundles in the car, and then we'll see if we can get your old bus on the way again."

After half an hour's experimenting with the faulty ignition, it was Phil who discovered the cause. One of the insulated wires connected to Bickerton's gadget had come adrift.

" You'd better remove the dial and connect up the wires," he suggested. " If not we'll be hanging about here for most of the night."

The remedy proved successful and soon the engine was humming softly. The two bundles of contraband were then dumped into the back of the car, only to provide a fresh problem: there was no room for Phil.

" He's only a lightweight," declared Bernard. " He can sit on my knee—or stand on the running-board if he thinks that more comfortable. But look here, Bickerton, you'd better cut out all ideas of spending the night in the rope-walk."

" Don't say that," rejoined the pressman in a disappointed tone. " Why?"

" For one thing, your precious gadget's out of order and it wouldn't be wise to leave your car on the road all night," explained Bradfield. " So you'd better drop us somewhere farther on, and then make for the Crab and Lobster. Then, after a good night's rest—which is more than Preston and I can expect—you can take your car to Bridport, hand the smuggled stuff over to the Customs—get them to examine it in your presence, mind!—and then be back in Brinkwater bright and early for your precious flower show!"

It was nearly midnight by the time the reporter's car drew up outside the eastern end of the rope-walk. Owing to the delay Bernard and Phil had decided not to leave their suitcases in the ruined cowshed but to carry on towards the scene of impending operations.

" The best of luck!" exclaimed Bickerton.

" And the same to you!" replied the chums.

The reporter turned the car round and drove off. Obligingly he was carrying out their wishes that he would make for Brinkwater by a circuitous route.

Left to their own devices, the chums effected an entry into the long wooden building by the same means and at the same spot as they had done on the previous night. What a lot seemed to have taken place since then!

They could but hope that the suspect would make another attempt and would not be deterred by the light of Jasper Nightingale's torch. It was most unlikely that the amateur fisherman would go down to the shore on two nights in succession. They hadn't expected him during their previous vigil, but all the same he had appeared upon the scene at a most inopportune time!

Taking up their previous places of concealment, the watchers began their uncomfortable yet tense vigil, straining their eyes to catch the first glimmer of a light from the far end of the rope-walk.

They were too far apart to talk to one another without raising their voices, although when once Phil did his best to stifle a cough the sound echoed along and under the low-pitched roof like a distant peal of thunder. They could not help envying Bickerton, who by this time was probably asleep in a comfortable bed at the Crab and Lobster, dreaming of the small fortune likely to come his way from His Majesty's Customs and Excise authorities!

One o'clock sounded from the mile-away Brinkwater church tower. Shortly afterwards a brisk westerly breeze sprang up. With it the wooden building began to creak and groan, while to add to these conditions of discomfort, rats started to scamper over the floor, and even on the beams overhead of the chums' places of concealment.

Again and again Phil consulted the luminous hands of his wrist-watch, guarding the face with a cupped hand lest even that feeble glimmer might betray his position. How slowly the minutes passed! More than once he held the watch to his ear to reassure himself that it had not stopped.

Then, suddenly and unexpectedly, the door nearest the footbridge over the recently manufactured rope opened with the creaking sound of rusty hinges.

The door was only about three yards from the spot where Phil was in hiding. Neither he nor Bernard had expected anyone—except perhaps Jasper Nightingale—to use that entry during the night hours. Perhaps it was Nightingale behaving in an eccentric manner. Some fishermen are like that, Phil thought.

But it wasn't Nightingale. It was a much taller man.

Phil lay perfectly quiet, afraid that even his breathing would betray him. Why hadn't the fellow—supposing that it were the same nocturnal visitor—come along the path from the Brinkwater end of the building as he had attempted to do on the preceding night, instead of using the entrance that was supposed to be for the sole use of people living in Sea View and Peacehaven?

Pausing to close the door behind him, the fellow passed Phil's place of concealment and, with the air of one accustomed to the locality, reached the steps of the recently repaired footbridge.

Then instead of crossing the trench by the bridge, he dropped down to the long trough along which lay the ropes, supported at regular intervals by grooved wheels.

Now, for the first time, he showed a light. It was only a little stronger than that of a domestic night-light, but there was sufficient reflected glimmer for Phil to recognize the man.

It was George Tankerton.

Quite probably Bernard had made a similar discovery, thought Phil. They should have come to some definite decision as to what ought to be done. Would Bradfield pounce upon the man, before he had definite proof that his actions were of a sinister nature? Phil hoped not. Apart from evidence it would be highly interesting to see what Tankerton was about.

Bradfield did remain silent and motionless. He, too, was awaiting developments until there could be no doubt concerning Tankerton's intentions.

The two air police officers hadn't much longer to wait.

Setting his lamp down on the side of the trench, Tankerton produced an object that looked very much like a long-spouted oil-can as used by engineers. He appeared to be removing a cap at the end of the nozzle, holding it closer to the light in order to see what he was doing.

It wasn't a metal container, but what was it made of? For the present Phil had to give that question up.

Bending over the four lines of rope, Tankerton squirted the cordage with some liquid from the instrument he was holding. Phil couldn't see what the fluid looked like, but by the sound it made as it left the spout, it was evident that it wasn't heavy oil. In all probability it was either nitric or sulphuric acid, diluted perhaps, yet sufficiently strong in delayed action seriously to impair the strength of any rope, irrespective of its size.

It was then that Bradfield took action.

" What do you think you're up to, Tankerton?" he demanded, switching on his torch as he challenged.

Almost at the same moment, Preston brought his electric torch into action.

Caught in the converging beams the saboteur must have been temporarily blinded by the glare. He looked to be on the point of hurling the acid container at the challenger nearest to him—which happened to be Bernard. Had he done so and had the cowardly missile reached its intended mark, Bernard might have been blinded for the rest of his life.

Probably thinking better of his intentions, Tankerton dropped the container to the floor of the trench, where it broke into several pieces. Then, still clutching his lamp, he took to his heels along the long narrow passage leading to the works office.

The chums started in pursuit, but quickly they became aware that, good runners though they were, Tankerton was outpacing them. They were still gamely continuing the chase when, in the darkness, Phil tripped over a pig of iron and measured his length on the ground.

Bernard stopped and went to his chum's assistance.

" Hurt?" he inquired laconically.

" I don't think so," replied Phil gamely, although he was painfully aware of a sprained ankle.
" Don't wait. Follow him up and nab him."

" No need for that," declared Bernard, glancing
at the manager's flying figure, for by now he'd
obtained a very useful lead of at least a hundred
yards. " We can let the local police get on with
that!"

" Supposing he does himself in?"

" In that case he won't commit any more acts
of sabotage," rejoined Bernard grimly.

" Or attempts to flee the country?"

" There again, it's a job for the Dorset
Constabulary or even Scotland Yard. Now you'd
better sit down and wait till I bring our suitcases
along. Then we'll see if we can effect an entry
into Sea View."

" We're both going to fetch those suitcases,"
declared Phil obstinately. " The walk will do my
ankle good."

" I don't see how."

" My theory is—and I've proved it—that
there are two directly opposite means of dealing
with a sprained foot," explained Phil. " One is
to lie up and rest it. The other is to keep on the
move. When I was a kid of about ten, I was
exploring a ruined castle. I slipped and fell about
twelve or fifteen feet. I well remember staggering
to my feet, feeling giddy, and flopping on the
grass again. There didn't seem anything else I
could do about it, so I tramped the whole way

home—a distance of seven miles. Long before I arrived there, I'd almost forgotten my sprained ankle."

By now they had returned to their recent place of concealment, Phil doing his best not to limp.

Switching on his torch, Bernard let himself drop into the shallow trench under the wooden footbridge. There he found what he was looking for—the remains of a shattered stoneware container still wet with the acid spilt from it. Some of the liquid had been forced between the strands of one of the ropes.

" H_2SO_4 without a shadow of doubt," he declared.

" Mind your fingers!" cautioned his chum.

" Trust me for that," rejoined Bernard. " We'll let someone else do the examination; but beyond a shadow of doubt, it's sulphuric acid that Tankerton's been using."

They retrieved their suitcases and then, taking to the road, made their way to the entrance to Sea View.

" Let's hope that the front door is on the latch," said Phil.

Their luck was out. The door was not only locked, it was bolted—a most unusual occurrence at Mrs. Marshbarrow's guest house.

There seemed to be only one thing to be done. That was to spend the rest of the night in the summer house until the front door of Sea View was opened at six o'clock.

It was now a fairly warm night. The chilly breeze had died down. It another two hours it would be dawn.

Resting comfortably in a couple of deck chairs, the chums felt no desire for sleep. In spite of the fact that, as police officers, they should keep cool and collected, they were approaching a pitch of excitement.

" What could have possessed Tankerton to act as he did, I wonder?" asked Phil. " It doesn't make sense for a manager to sabotage the property in his charge. Do you think it's a case of dual personality? Is he a sort of Jekyll and Hyde?"

" We don't know," replied his companion. " Whatever the reason, he went about the job in a very cunning way. But we fixed him when we let him—and others—know that we were leaving Brinkwater for a few days. Did it ever occur to you that Tankerton might be a foreigner?"

" What makes you think that?" asked Phil. " I haven't noticed any foreign accent in his manner of speech."

" Neither have I," admitted Bernard. " But supposing he is a foreigner, it's just possible that he's under the thumb of a sort of saboteur-in-chief. There are fellows of that sort in this country. The Yard has plenty of evidence of that, but it's difficult to get the principal men. They leave their actual sabotage to their dupes. My conviction is that Tankerton, whether he's a foreigner

G 553

" What do you think you are up to, Tankerton?"
he demanded

or not, has been blackmailed into doing what he's done."

They continued to discuss the matter.

"Having discovered the identity of the saboteur—in a way I feel sorry for him—the only thing we can do is to ring up the Bridport police and let them get on with it," suggested Bradfield.

"But we'll be wanted as witnesses at the trial."

"They haven't arrested Tankerton yet," Bernard pointed out. "Of course we may not be required at his preliminary appearance before the local magistrates. I won't be sorry to be back at Hawkscar."

"We'll report to Standish by telephone and see what he says," rejoined his chum. "But as to returning to Hawkscar, there's one thing you've overlooked."

"And that is——?" prompted Bradfield.

"The circumstances under which we crashed H.104, my lad!"

Soon after six o'clock, when various signs and noises proclaimed that another day had begun at Sea View, Bernard and Phil left their temporary shelter. Neither felt any the worse for their lack of sleep, while Phil declared—mendaciously—that his sprained ankle was a thing of the past.

The front door of Sea View was now open. They went in to be confronted by the proprietress.

" Whoever expected to see you at this time!" she exclaimed. " I thought you said you wouldn't be coming back before Saturday!"

" Not later than Saturday, Mrs. Marsh-barrow," amended Bernard. " We're early, we know, but that we can't help. Now will you be a friend to man? We want hot baths, followed by a big breakfast at, say, a quarter to eight."

" I'll see," replied Mrs. Marshbarrow, non-committally; but, from experience, the chums knew that when she said " I'll see ", both baths and a meal would be forthcoming. " Have you been arresting anybody since you've been away?"

" Not that we're aware of," replied Bernard, not at all taken aback by the question: for by now it seemed to be common knowledge in

Brinkwater that Mrs. Marshbarrow was " doing for " a couple of detectives!

" It's no use ringing up Chief Inspector Standish before nine," said Phil, at the conclusion of their satisfying meal—that incidentally included a couple of freshly caught lobsters. " But it won't be a bad idea if we phone the Bridport police. We should have done so in the small hours of the morning."

There was no telephone at Sea View. The nearest one was at a call-box not far from the offices of the Brinkwater Rope Walk.

They got through to Bridport and made a brief report to the police officer in charge, and were told that a couple of officers would be upon the scene at ten o'clock.

It was now twenty minutes to nine. It was of little use to attempt to put a trunk call through to Hawkscar before nine, the hour when Chief Inspector Colin Standish would arrive at his office.

" We can fill in some of the time by inquiring at the works if Tankerton's there," suggested Bernard. " I don't suppose he will be there, but the foreman may be able to give us some information as to his whereabouts."

" Mr. Tankerton isn't here yet," replied the elderly foreman, who knew, from their previous visits, the names—and most likely the profession— of the callers. " He's usually here dead on the stroke of eight."

" He's not away for the day?" asked Phil.

" Oh no, sir. He wouldn't do that without
letting me know beforehand. He'll be detained
at his house belike. There's smoke coming from
one of the chimneys, so I reckon he can't be far
away from home."

The foreman pointed to the tall narrow building
where Tankerton lived. From one of the chimneys
a cloud of smoke was emerging—an indication
that someone, probably Tankerton himself, had
just " stoked up ".

Soon after nine Bernard obtained his trunk call
to the Royal Air Constabulary district headquarters at Hawkscar. The operator there
switched through to Standish's private office.

Briefly, Bernard made his report.

" You've done very well," observed Standish.
" You'd better remain at Brinkwater until the
local magistrates send the accused to the Assizes.
By the way, where did you leave the damaged
helicopter?"

" At Bere Regis Aerodrome, sir."

Bernard thought he heard a chuckle. His
chief, he knew, had a personal interest in that
establishment. In common with Phil Preston
and Bernard himself, Standish had started on
his air career there.

" I won't ask what you were doing there,"
observed Standish. " We'll presume it was in
connection with the case you were engaged upon.
That being so, the cost of repairs to the helicopter

will be borne out of police funds. That's all for
the present. Let me know of any further developments. Cheerio!"

" We haven't to pay for the damage to H.104,
my festive!" exclaimed Bernard, after his chief had
rung off. " It's jolly decent of Standish. We
might have been badly in the *consommé*."

It certainly had been a load on their mind. It
had been lurking there far too long. Later there
would be the usual court of inquiry into the
mishap to the helicopter, but, with their chief's
assurance that they would not be called upon to
pay for repairs out of their own pockets, they
could face that with equanimity.

Before Phil could express his thoughts upon
the matter the stillness of the morning air was
shattered by the raucous wail of Brinkwater's fire
alarm. It wasn't the first time that the chums
had heard that!

" Where now, I wonder!" exclaimed Bernard.
" It looks as if Charles Bickerton will have something else to attend besides his flower show."

" Look! There it is!" declared Phil excitedly.

Tankerton's house was on fire.

The smoke from the chimney was shooting up
in a dense black and brownish cloud. That was
not all. From the windows in the first storey
flames were issuing. So rapidly had the conflagration obtained a hold that it certainly looked as if
it were due to the use of petrol or some other
highly inflammable liquid.

" Good heavens!" ejaculated Bradfield. " Surely he hasn't chosen that way out?"

The chums ran towards the burning house. They were by no means the first to arrive. Men, women and children gathered outside to gaze with awe upon the scene. There was nothing much they could do, although a couple of fishermen—one of them Cranston, the owner of *Ripple* —had burst open the front door and were dragging articles of furniture into the street. Until the arrival of the local fire-fighters little else could be done; while before the flames could be got well under control the brigade from Bridport would have to be summoned.

With commendable promptitude Brinkwater's firemen arrived upon the scene, bringing hoses —which might prove to be worse than useless in dealing with blazing petrol—and a few chemical fire extinguishers.

Before the men could go into action, shouts broke from the lips of many of the onlookers. Arms were raised and fingers pointed at the roof.

Leaning out of one of the windows of the top storey was a man shouting for help.

In spite of his dishevelled appearance and his smoke-blackened face, the chums recognized him.

It was George Tankerton.

Had it been his intention to destroy himself in the flames? Had his resolution failed him at the last moment? Was his appeal too late?

Apparently it was too late. No fireman, however

determined, could hope to force his way up the
fiercely burning staircases and bring the threatened
man down to safety.   And Brinkwater's fire-
fighters did not possess an " escape ".   By the
time Bridport's brigade arrived upon the scene
it would be too late.

Suddenly the open upstairs window was empty.
A groan went up from many of the onlookers.
Almost everyone—and that included Bernard and
Phil—thought that the trapped man had been
overcome by the smoke and fumes and had
collapsed upon the floor.

But he appeared again, carrying something on
his left shoulder that turned out to be a coil of
rope.   This he partly uncoiled; then with a
professional overhand cast he hurled most of the
rope into the air.

The end of the coil dropped within a couple
of yards from the spot where the chums were
standing.   They, with others, grasped it.

" Take up the strain!" shouted the trapped man
in a high-pitched voice, so different from the suave
tones he used in ordinary conversation.

" Gently, now!" exclaimed one of the firemen.
" Not too much strain!   I reckon he's got the
end made fast to a bed or something like that!"

The contradictory caution was not only obvious
but necessary.   With too many people pulling too
lustily on the rope, the object to which it was
attached might give and the rope would be jerked
uselessly upon the heads and shoulders of the

throng. Apart from that, the rope—apparently made of three-inch manilla—was not likely to break under even a much greater strain.

With an agility that made Phil think that at one period of his career he had been a sailor, Tankerton swung himself over the window-sill, threw his legs over the tautened rope, gripped it with both hands and allowed his body to be suspended under what looked like being, literally, his line of retreat.

At this stage of the proceedings an inexperienced man would probably let the rope slip through his hands, with the result that he would land on the ground with broken legs.

Not so Tankerton.

Hand under hand—it was climbing in reverse —he began the descent, slowly and apparently confidently.

He was still about twenty or twenty-five feet from the ground when calamity overtook him.

The rope suddenly parted, just above his head. To the chums it looked as if he were gliding, with arms outstretched, towards the ground, though actually his rate of descent was almost as fast as that of a dropped stone. He fell heavily on his back within ten feet of where Bernard and Phil were holding the now slack end of the broken rope.

They went to his assistance. So did a First Aid man, and some of the onlookers.

Tankerton's face was a pale, ghastly hue.

A trickle of blood was oozing from his lips. His eyes were wide open. He was still conscious.

" Best not touch him till we get a stretcher," suggested the ambulance worker. " One of you fetch Doctor Simpson; and stand back you others and give him air."

He bent over the injured man.

" Much pain, sir?" he asked.

" No; can't feel any," was the reply.

The First Aid man stood up and addressed Preston. Evidently he, like many of the crowd, had a vague idea who Phil and Bernard were. The common belief seemed to be that they were Scotland Yard officers.

" He's done for, I reckon," he declared. " Absence of pain: that looks like severe spinal injuries to me."

There seemed nothing that the chums could do. Somewhat helplessly they remained, knowing that they could do little or nothing until after the doctor had arrived upon the scene.

Then, without turning his head, Tankerton looked and recognized Phil.

" I want to speak—to you," he said, audibly and distinctly, although with an obvious effort.

Phil crouched beside him, while Bernard stood behind his chum. Some of the crowd surged nearer, only to be sternly ordered to stand back by the somewhat pompous First Aid man. Now was his chance to exercise his authority and he was taking full advantage of it.

" What is it?" prompted Preston.

" You've won!" declared the injured man.

" Don't let's talk about that now," urged Phil.

" I must—it's on my mind—I'm going, I know that, but before then——"

His voice trailed away to silence. Phil thought that he was passing out, but again Tankerton opened his eyes.

" Blackmailed!" he murmured audibly. " For years—Zensky—calls himself Brownly—remember the name, Zensky—in the safe in the cellar —keys in trousers pocket—you take them out —Zensky will be here—Monday about eleven."

Again after muttering unintelligibly his voice died away.

However much he disliked disturbing the obviously fatally injured man, Phil slid his hand into his pocket and withdrew a bunch of keys.

Tankerton remained motionless. He was now beginning to breathe with obvious difficulty. He was incapable of further speech.

" I want you, if necessary, to bear witness that these keys were taken by me at Mr. Tankerton's request," said Phil, addressing the First Aid man.

Just then the local doctor arrived upon the scene, followed within half a minute by the Red Cross ambulance. After Doctor Simpson had given him a shot of morphia, four pairs of practised hands lifted Tankerton on a stretcher and loaded him into the ambulance.

" That's the last we shall see of him, poor fellow!" remarked Phil.

" It seems like it," agreed Bernard. " And now he's left us with another problem: what shall we find in his safe?"

The arrival of the efficient and up-to-date fire brigade from the neighbouring town quickly completed the praiseworthy efforts of Brinkwater's fire-fighters.

Before then, Bernard had retrieved the severed parts of the rope and, having cut them away, made a quick inspection of the strands.

" It looks as if Tankerton has been ' hoist by his own petard '," he observed to his chum. " I don't suppose for one moment that he had the slightest idea that the rope had been doctored when he used it as a way of escape."

" And what did he mean when he mentioned blackmail and Zensky? And something about Monday."

" I have an idea, but what it's worth remains to be seen," replied Bernard. " It depends upon what's in that safe, and we won't be able to do anything about it until the house has cooled down. Or even longer than that if the floors have collapsed. But searching amongst the debris isn't our job. We'll have to hand that over to the Dorset Constabulary."

" I suppose so," agreed Phil reluctantly. " All

the same, I'd like to see this part of the affair through."

"You will," declared his companion confidently. "The police will be glad of whatever assistance we can give, especially if Monday at eleven means anything. Somehow I feel that it will! Did you hear Tankerton muttering something after ' Monday about eleven '?"

"I did," admitted Phil, "but I couldn't make head or tail of it."

"Neither could I," agreed his brother officer. "It wasn't German but it was in some foreign tongue —Ha! Here come the police—slightly too late for their intended job, I fancy!"

A covered van had just drawn up. There was nothing painted on it to give any indication that it was a constabulary vehicle, but above the windscreen was an illuminated word: *Police*.

From the vehicle alighted a sergeant and two constables, leaving another policeman as driver.

By this time the fire had not only been extinguished but there was no sign of its breaking out again. The damage now seemed to have been confined to the first floor. Except for the broken windows there was little, as seen from the road, to indicate that there had been a serious conflagration

"You're too late, sergeant," declared Bernard, after he had made himself known.

"So it seems, sir," rejoined the sergeant. "Were there any signs of Tankerton?"

"Yes, he's been removed to hospital. I very much doubt if he'll recover. Hullo! Here's Bickerton! You've met Bickerton before to-day, sergeant?"

"I have that," replied Sergeant Brown of the Dorset Constabulary.

"I'm a bit late," declared the *Evening Monitor's* reporter. "I've only just got away from the Customs and Excise people at Bridport. I didn't do too badly there! But what's happened here?"

"Something more exciting than your precious flower show," replied Phil. "Tankerton was trapped. He tried to escape from the fire but injured himself badly. It seems almost certain that he won't pull through."

"Then Sergeant Brown has come all this way for nothing," observed the reporter.

"Far from it," declared Phil. "We're about to make a discovery that will put Tankerton's delinquencies in the shade. You can have a hand in it too, Bickerton!"

"What's all this, sir?" inquired Sergeant Brown, slightly put out by not having already been informed of the nature of the discovery.

Phil told him of his disjointed conversation with the badly injured Tankerton.

"Directly the firemen say it's safe to do so, we'll explore the cellar," he added. "You're included in the search-party, Bickerton, only not a word about this in your paper until Tuesday!"

They continued to discuss the situation for

about another half-hour, until they were told by the captain of the fire brigade that they could enter the building—but at their own risk.

By this time only about half a dozen onlookers remained. Perhaps they were curious to know what the police were about to do. The firemen, too, were " packing up ", although they were leaving one of their number on duty inside the damaged house in case there might be a fresh outbreak.

The search-party consisted of the sergeant and one constable, the representative of the press and the two sub-inspectors from far off Hawkscar.

Although the house showed little signs of damage when viewed from the street—a casual passer-by would fail to notice that there had been a fire—the ceiling of the ground floor was sagging badly as the result of water seeping through from the rooms above. The brigade, having put out the fire by means of chemical extinguishers, had made doubly sure against a subsequent flare-up by deluging the floors with water.

" Where is the way down to the cellar?" asked the police sergeant.

" We don't know," replied Bernard. " We haven't been in this house before."

They searched and found nothing resembling a doorway to lead to the cellar.

" Perhaps Tankerton's mind was wandering when he mentioned a cellar," suggested the pressman.

"He told me where to find the key, anyway," declared Phil. "Let's look under the carpet."

They shifted a large table to one side of the room and rolled back the sodden carpet. There was no ringbolt or metal fastening to suggest the presence of a trap-door, but close to one of the inner walls they discovered that four adjacent floor-boards had been cut through in two places about four feet apart.

Bernard stooped to inspect the boards. Along one edge were marks of a recent attempt to prise them up.

"We'll want a chisel or a strong knife for this job," he declared.

Just then the fireman left on guard came into the room.

"What caused the fire, do you know?" asked Sergeant Brown.

"I don't just know, sergeant," replied the fireman. "But we did find a lot of charred paper and the remains of a petrol can in the room above. I reckon the bloke living here was burning documents for some reason and used petrol in mistake for paraffin. Quite a number of fools do that every day!"

Bernard looked round at his chum.

Did it mean that Tankerton's mind had been wandering when he spoke of the mysterious Zensky and the equally mysterious something in the safe in the cellar? Had he destroyed by fire whatever documents he had hidden there?

" What are you trying to do, sir?" asked the fireman. " Trying to lift them boards? Let me have a go!"

He removed a hatchet from his belt and inserted the keen edge between the ends of two adjacent boards. Then, having driven the blade still farther by stamping upon its back, he levered the axe until the boards—four in all—were raised and removed to reveal a rough wooden ladder. At one side of it was an electric switch. It was out of action as the result of the recent fire.

None of the party had a light apart from boxes of matches and a petrol lighter—illuminations totally inadequate to deal with the darkness of the cellar. There was no fanlight nor any method of ventilation, but the fire overhead had evidently set up an induced draught that had rendered the air in the cellar quite fresh.

There was some delay while the constable went to the police vehicle and returned with a couple of electric torches. Thus provided, the party, including the fireman who had deserted his post to see what the rest were about to do, descended into the vault-like cellar.

The safe was in the wall facing the ladder. Apparently it was of ancient vintage, for the metal door was rusty and corroded. It could easily be forced open without having to make use of a key.

At the third attempt Phil found the right key. The door opened easily—an indication that it had been recently used. In the safe was a leather-bound book that proved to be a diary and a bundle of papers held together by a rubber band.

"Wouldn't fetch sixpence at a jumble sale," declared Sergeant Brown contemptuously. "You'd better take charge of them, sir. If there is anything important perhaps you'll get in touch with my superintendent."

The party then left the house to separate. The police boarded their van, while Phil and Bernard, accompanied by Bickerton, set off towards Sea View.

"How did the flower show come off?" inquired Bernard of the pressman.

"I don't know," replied Bickerton. "I was most of the morning at Bridport seeing the Customs people; then on my way back here I heard the fire alarm, so I hurried along to see where it was. The flower show could jolly well wait!"

"How did you get on with the Customs people?" asked Phil.

"Not so dusty, although it might be better. Those two bundles were chock-full with tobacco and a tidy bit of snuff. They reckoned they were worth three hundred pounds and that I'll get ten per cent for finding it. That's forty quid, so after you've had your shares——"

The chums vigorously shook their heads, somewhat to the surprise and amusement of a woman who happened to be passing.

"We've already told you that it's your own

pidgin," declared Bernard. " That's settled. But there's one other matter. You'll be reporting on the fire at Tankerton's house? Use your discretion, but don't, whatever you do, mention anything about the mysterious Zensky or his probable visit to Brinkwater next Monday."

" Agreed!" declared the reporter.

" Splendid!" continued Bernard. " And I'll promise you this: if there's a show on on Monday, I'll see you get a front row of the stalls!"

Bernard and Phil, accompanied by Bickerton, returned to Sea View for a somewhat belated meal. It was already two o'clock and there were no signs of lunch being forthcoming. Mrs. Marshbarrow and most of her paying guests, including Jasper Nightingale, had taken advantage of the free entertainment provided by the fire. Although Mrs. Marshbarrow had returned home before the chums had, it was quite evident that the time-table at Sea View was considerably in arrear.

" I'm sorry for having asked you to come along with us for grub only to find it's not ready," said Bernard apologetically. " Let's hope you are not hungry."

" I'm used to meals at any odd time," replied Bickerton. " So don't worry on my account."

" While we're waiting we might have a go at Tankerton's papers," suggested Phil.

" Good idea!" agreed Bernard. " I'm glad we'll be able to have first cut at them. I was on tenterhooks, after we'd found them, that Sergeant Brown would take possession of them."

" Well, he hasn't," added the reporter. " He

failed in his duty, of course, and he's not the only one to do so."

They began with the bound journal. Actually the first hundred pages couldn't be termed that, since they were written in 1946. It was a personal narrative from Tankerton's late teens until his discharge from the forces at the conclusion of the war.

According to it he was a Pole, born at Labiau, a small fishing port on the shores of the Kurisches Haff, in the year 1920. There he was apprenticed to a fishing-net and rope manufacturer. When, in 1939, his country was simultaneously invaded by Germany and Russia, he was one of the defenders of Warsaw. On its fall he contrived to flee from Poland, going first to Sweden and then, by way of Norway, to Britain. Here he joined the newly formed Polish Brigade until the end of hostilities, in 1945. By this time he could speak and write English fluently, and in that same year he became a naturalized British subject. Shortly afterwards he obtained the post of branch manager of a rope-walk in Yorkshire, where he attracted the notice of Sir Montague Corton, who, according to the writer, was unaware of his original nationality. Before then he had abandoned his birth-name—Basil Vasilkov—for that of Tankerton.

After six months in Yorkshire, Tankerton was transferred to Brinkwater as manager, and at this stage the narrative ended.

" There's nothing there to show that he was a saboteur," remarked Bickerton. " It's quite obvious that he held a very good opinion of himself. So far he has recorded nothing to bring him within the clutches of the law."

" British law," amended Phil. " After what's written there it would have meant execution or life imprisonment had he returned to the Poland of to-day."

The bundle of papers dealt with a different matter—the circumstances under which Tankerton had fallen into the clutches of an organized gang of alien saboteurs, who aimed at hampering, if not wrecking, Britain's war effort. Why Tankerton had run the risk of writing them—for had they fallen into the hands of either the police or of the unprincipled alien gang, the result would have been much the same—had to remain something of a mystery until, recovered from the injuries, he would have to stand his trial.

But would he?

The method by which this mainly foreign organization got Tankerton into its clutches was described at considerable length. Each fresh development was chronicled soon after it had taken place. There was no attempt made to conceal names. Probably Tankerton had written with the object of letting this information fall into the hands of the authorities after his death in order to reveal the identities of his blackmailing masters.

For blackmailers they undoubtedly were, besides being master saboteurs. One of the names that struck Bradfield and Preston almost at once was Zensky. It occurred several times. He was the fellow who had first tricked Tankerton into committing an act of indiscretion. Gradually he got his victim into his clutches. The wretched man had been forced to sabotage the works of which he was manager.

Zensky had visited Brinkwater Rope Walk on several occasions mainly—as Tankerton made a point of noting in his papers—to upbraid him for his timidity and to force him to greater efforts.

"Poor blighter!" exclaimed Bickerton. "He must have been having a sticky time. Did you have any suspicion that he was a foreigner?"

"Not until he muttered something after he'd mentioned Zensky, just before he was taken away by the ambulance," replied Phil. "And Zensky's coming to pay him a visit next Monday at two."

"At eleven," amended Bernard.

"That makes matters worse, then," continued his chum. "To-day's Saturday. That leaves only one clear day."

"For what?"

"To make plans to catch Zensky."

"That's not our business," declared Bernard. "All we can do is to inform the county police and let them get on with it."

"When are you sending in your report of the fire, Bickerton?" asked Phil.

" To-night," replied the pressman.

" If Zensky should chance to see it he'll cancel his visit to Brinkwater," Phil pointed out.

Bickerton gave another of his cheerful grins.

" Wrong there!" he exclaimed. " We don't publish a Sunday edition. The report won't appear until noon on Monday. But the police will have to see to it that Zensky doesn't see that the house has been on fire. If he does he'll drive away, and as no one about here has a photo or even a description of him——"

" They'll throw a cordon round the place, stop all cars and question their drivers."

" I must be on the spot for that," declared Bickerton.

" And we'll be somewhere around—not too close," added Bernard. " It's not our pidgin, as we said, but it will be both interesting and gratifying to see the darbies clapped on Zensky—I say, Phil, perhaps it will be a good thing if we slip over to Bridport and see the police inspector there."

" Quite!" agreed Preston.

" Then let me run you over in my car," offered Bickerton. " And I'll bring you back. That's all on my way to Dorchester."

" To send in your copy?" asked Phil, with a smile.

" You've said it," rejoined the reporter.

"And now for lunch!" exclaimed Bernard, as Mrs. Marshbarrow appeared with a heavily laden

tray. " Or high tea, seeing that it's nearly four
o'clock."

" Couldn't get it ready no quicker," announced
the proprietress of Sea View. " Electricity cut or
something. But better late than never."

The three men had barely started on their long
overdue meal—in spite of culinary drawbacks
Mrs. Marshbarrow had again risen to the occasion—when Jenkins, the local police constable
was announced.

" I thought you'd like to know," he announced.
" I was on the rota to watch by Mr. Tankerton's
bed in case he came to and made a statement. I
was to have gone on at midnight, but the sergeant
rang through, ten minutes ago, to say I wouldn't
be needed."

" Why?" asked Phil.

He guessed what the answer would be. So did
his companions.

" Mr. Tankerton died at fifteen-thirty without
recovering consciousness, sir," replied Jenkins.

As soon as they had finished their delayed repast the three men set off for Bridport.

Although sorry about Tankerton's death, they could not help feeling that it was for the best. He would not have to stand his trial, doubtless to be condemned to a long term of imprisonment. There was another aspect on the matter that caused Bernard and Phil no slight cause for satisfaction. They would not now have to attend the Assizes, although they fully expected to have to be called as witnesses at the inquest of the late manager of the sabotaged rope-walk. But, they decided, having to appear at a coroner's inquiry was better than having to attend, perhaps for several days, a Court of Assizes.

They had also made up their minds not to be directly involved in any action the county police might take to arrest the so far elusive Zensky. All they meant to do was to hand Tankerton's diary and papers over to the inspector at Bridport, and let him get on with it. They meant, however, to obtain a view, from a discreet distance, of the probable meeting between the representatives of the law and the mysterious Zensky.   They didn't know his fore-name; they were unaware of his nationality, although it would be safe to assume that he was either a Russian or a Soviet dominated Pole.

Whatever nationality he might be, there could be little or no doubt that—to quote Bickerton—he was a dirty piece of work.

Bickerton slowed down as he drove his car past Tankerton's house. His passengers were able to have a fairly good view of the front of it. Although the fire had played havoc with most of the interior, the roof appeared to be intact. The glass in one window had been smashed, but it would require a very sharp pair of eyes to detect any traces of burning. Zensky could drive right up to the building without realizing that the interior had been nearly gutted.

At Bridport they stopped outside the post office. The chums went in to send off a priority telegram to their chief. Phil wrote on the form:

" Suspect B detected. Died in hospital as result of fire. Preston, Bradfield."

" That won't do," objected Bernard.

" Why not?" asked his friend.

" ' As result of fire.' That might read as if he'd been shot."

Phil agreed. He could well imagine Chief Inspector Colin Standish enjoying his usual early evening round of golf—Saturday was generally his day for that—and being interrupted by a messenger handing him a telegram stating that

" Suspect B " was dead as the result of fire.
There could be two interpretations to that!

" Then, ' as the result of accidental injuries '.
That should do the trick," amended Phil. " And
we'd better add, ' Report follows '."

From the post office they went to the police
station.

" Come on in with us, Bickerton," said Bernard.
" I don't suppose the inspector will raise any
objections to you in your professional capacity."

" Inspector Protheroe knows me all right,"
rejoined the reporter. " He and I are quite good
friends. There's mutual understanding between
the police and the press in this part of the country!"

They found Inspector Protheroe in his office,
engaged in studying a document.

" I'm looking at Sergeant Brown's report," he
announced, after preliminary courtesies had been
exchanged. " I am by no means convinced that
Tankerton—a respected figure in this district—
was guilty of sabotage."

" Perhaps these documents will convince you,
sir," said Phil, placing Tankerton's autobiography
and the incriminating papers on his desk. " We'll
leave them with you. Some concern a foreigner
living in this country—Zensky's his name."

" Never heard of the fellow," declared the
inspector. " Who is he? What is he?"

Briefly Phil told all he knew about the man:
of the references made to him in Tankerton's
papers and how, soon after receiving injuries that

had since proved to be fatal, Tankerton had managed to reveal that Zensky was coming to Brinkwater to see him at eleven o'clock on the following Monday.

" At eleven a.m. or eleven p.m.?"

Preston couldn't give a definite answer. He just didn't know!

The injured Tankerton, in his last conscious moments, had made an indefinite statement, and Phil, listening to him, hadn't noticed its vagueness.

" I really don't know, sir," he admitted.

The inspector could have shot at him a look of withering scorn. He didn't.

" Then if the morning rendezvous isn't kept we must be prepared for a spot of night work," he observed. " My personal view is that the fellow will arrive at Tankerton's house at or about eleven at night. 'They prefer darkness to light because their deeds are evil' is a statement made nineteen hundred years ago that still holds good to-day."

" We brought these along in case you might be interested," said Bernard, opening a leather case he had brought with him.

From it he produced four short lengths of rope. Two of them were in clean condition; the others had been smeared by mud and discoloured by smoke.

" These two ends I cut from one of the ropes that Tankerton was dosing in the rope-walk," he explained. " The others came from the rope that apparently broke under his weight when he attempted to escape from his burning house. The break in each case was caused by acid action."

"This is decidedly interesting," declared the inspector, as he gingerly handled and examined the cordage. "But I still just can't see why Tankerton trusted himself to a rope that he knew to be defective through his own action. I'll take charge of the specimens and have them sent to our physical laboratory for testing. That's all for the present. I'll go through these documents before I turn in to-night. I'd like to see you both, and you too, Bickerton—I know we can rely upon your discretion—say at two o'clock to-morrow."

He placed the diary and the papers that went with it in a drawer. On the top of them he put the short lengths of rope. Then he escorted his callers to Bickerton's car.

"It looks as if we're going to be brought into the affair whether we want to or not," remarked Bernard. "I'd be quite content to watch developments from a reasonable distance."

It did not take them long to return to Brinkwater. Bickerton set them down outside Sea View and drove off for Dorchester, promising to call for Bernard and Phil at half-past one on the next day.

The chums were only too glad to be able to turn in early. They had had a decidedly strenuous time. They were too tired even to think of writing out their detailed reports for Chief Inspector Colin Standish.

It was nearly ten in the morning before they awoke. Bernard had just finished shaving when he chanced to glance at the leather case that he had left on the window-ledge.

It didn't look the same as it had done previously. The leather was stained a greyish hue, as if it had been splashed with salt water.

He opened the case. The lining had been partly eaten away by some corrosive substance.

" What do you make of this, Phil?" he asked.

" Make of what?"

" The case, of course!"

Preston looked at it.

" Why, it's been eaten through by some sort of acid!" he exclaimed. " It must have come from those bits of rope—delayed action of sorts."

" It certainly does look like it," agreed Bernard. " And the inspector put the rope in a drawer of his desk with Tankerton's papers. If there's any potent acid still left in the rope-ends it will play up with them. The case is done for. We'd better throw it out somewhere in the garden."

" That won't do," objected his chum. " Mrs. Marshbarrow's cats might have a go at it, with dire results to them. No, better cart the remains back to Bridport and let the police analyst have a cut at it."

" Let's hope it hasn't damaged the upholstery of Bickerton's car," said Bernard.

Before they had their belated breakfast—which they decided would also serve for lunch—they took the corroded bag out into the garden and placed it in a conveniently sized box. They would take it with them on their trip to Bridport.

Bickerton arrived with his car, but an examination showed that, so far, no damage had been done to the vehicle.

" It's a dirty trick," declared the pressman. " Almost as bad as a delayed-action bomb. I wonder what Inspector Protheroe will say when he knows about it."

But Inspector Protheroe knew about it already.

" You're telling me!" he exclaimed when, an hour later, the trio were seated in his inner office. " I waded half-way through Tankerton's papers last night before putting them back in that drawer, with the doctored ropes underneath. When I took them out at nine this morning, intending to finish reading them, I found them badly messed up by some sort of acid."

" Are they readable?" asked Bickerton.

" It's doubtful. I told Sergeant Baker to put them into a solution of vinegar and water. That might do the trick. It's something new to me—a delayed-action acid. Our lab. staff will be interested."

" We've brought the remains of the leather case," announced Bernard, indicating the wooden box he had placed on the floor by the side of his chair.

" I don't want to see it!" declared the inspector.

All the same, he peered into the box and then, ringing for the station sergeant, told him to take it across to the laboratory.

" And are those papers dry yet?" he asked.

" Getting on that way, sir," replied Baker. " Though I have my doubts whether we'll be able to read most of them."

Having finished—at least for the time being—with the box and its decidedly dangerous contents, Inspector Protheroe proceeded to explain the steps he proposed taking against the expected appearance of the still somewhat mysterious Zensky.

" It's quite possible he goes under another name—probably a good old Scots one," he observed, as he unfolded a large-scale map of Brinkwater on the table. " He'll arrive by car— that's pretty certain. Now we'll assume that he comes by the Dorchester road. Here's Tankerton's house—I'm stationing a heavy lorry down this side street, about fifty yards away. If a car draws up outside the house a constable will request to see the occupant's identity cards and also the driver's licence. Should he have any cause for suspicion he'll give a blast on his whistle, and immediately the lorry will be run across the road to prevent the car from getting away. I'll have half a dozen of my men ready, and we'll pounce upon friend Zensky in almost less than no time."

"Supposing he turns the car round and tears off by the road he came?" asked Phil.

"Not at all likely," replied the inspector. "A car, even with a short wheel-base, couldn't turn in the width of the road. He would have to back and then go ahead at least twice."

"But he might back the car, perhaps for a couple of hundred yards, and then turn before your men could be on the spot," suggested Bernard.

Protheroe smiled. He didn't altogether like his plans being criticized by two junior officers of the Royal Air Constabulary.

"Perhaps you two would like to take steps to cut off Zensky's retreat if he tries to do so by the Dorchester road," suggested the inspector.

"That's not part of our duty, sir," Phil rejoined. "Our orders were to detect the saboteur at the rope-walk. That we've done. Now we've arranged, with Mr. Bickerton, to wait here "—he pointed out the position on the map—" and watch proceedings from a reasonable distance."

"But you are forgetting one thing," Protheroe reminded him. "That is that it's the duty of every citizen to assist the police when called upon by them to do so. The fact that you are in the Air Constabulary does not affect the case."

"You're right," agreed Phil, and his chum nodded in silent agreement. Now that they were to be something more than passive onlookers, they might just as well enter into the spirit of the thing.

"As you are not proposing to set up a road-block at the eastern end of Brinkwater, have you any objection to our arranging to have one, sir?" asked Bernard. "That is just in case the fellow does happen to avoid the trap you are setting!"

"What sort of road-block do you suggest?" asked the inspector.

"There's a mechanical grab engaged in clearing a dyke between the main road and the rope-walk."

"Yes," agreed Protheroe, "I've seen it at work there."

"We could get the driver to lower the arm of his crane and swing it across the road. It's quite long enough for that. Nothing in the nature of a wheeled vehicle could pass; and it would be a matter of a few seconds to swing it clear when we've finished with it."

"Very well," agreed the inspector. "But see that every precaution is taken against a bona-fide road user being injured. I won't hold myself responsible if that happens! I think that's all for the present. I want everyone concerned to be at their posts by ten in the morning, in case Zensky puts in an appearance before the expected time. And," he concluded with a smile, "I hope it will be in the morning and not at eleven o'clock at night!"

Monday morning dawned grey and misty—an indication that, once the sun broke through, the day would be warm and bright.

Bernard and Phil were up soon after six and, an hour later, Bickerton, who had spent the night at his home in Dorchester, arrived, accompanied by one of the staff photographers of the *Evening Monitor*, an alert-looking fellow of about eighteen or nineteen.

"I hope you don't mind me bringing Fuller along," said Bickerton. "A few good snaps would make quite a lot of difference."

"I suppose they would," admitted Bernard, although, he thought, it would have been better had Bickerton given the chums warning of his intention on the previous day. Fuller might have talked indiscreetly with some of his colleagues.

Bickerton must have read Bradfield's thoughts.

"I've dragged Fuller down on false pretences," he declared. "He doesn't know now what he's been let in for. He thinks it's to take pictures of an athletic meeting—don't you, Fuller?"

"We may be mixed up with some form of athletics before the day's done," said Phil gravely.

" We don't think for one moment that there'll be bullets flying about; but one never knows."

Briefly the press photographer was informed of the state of affairs in Brinkwater, that led up to Tankerton's death and the expected visit of the blackmailer, Zensky. There was no need to bind Fuller to secrecy. Nothing he could do or say could influence the course of events of the day.

" Are you armed?" he asked.

" No fear!" replied Bernard emphatically. " Nor are the county police. The use of firearms by the police went out of fashion after the Sidney Street affair. That's well before your time—and ours. If Protheroe's plans are successful, Zensky will have the bracelets on him before he can draw his gun—if he carries one."

" You'd better leave your car in the grounds here, Bickerton," suggested Bernard. " The fewer cars the better on this game. We'll walk. Let's hope that our friend the mechanical grab expert isn't taking a day off!"

Bradfield's fears were groundless.

The grab was hard at it as the four men approached. It had been daily on the job for nearly a month, clearing out and deepening a dyke between the rope-walk and the public road. It was now operating opposite the main entrance to the works and about one hundred and fifty yards from the house so lately occupied by the deceased manager.

The grab descended into the slime with a

gurgling noise and a metallic clatter. Usually
there was a brief interval of comparative silence
before the bucket reappeared to deposit its contents on the adjoining ground.

As he usually did, the operator waved a greeting
to the chums. This time Bickerton and Fuller
were included in the friendly gesture.

" Can we have a word with you?" asked
Bernard, taking advantage of the lull.

" Sure!"

The operator leant out of his cab. Only ten or
twelve feet separated him from the road.

Briefly and concisely Bernard told him what he
wanted to be done.

The cheery smile on the man's face died away.
In his ten years' employment by the Dorset
County Council he'd been asked to do a good
many things but never one like this.

" It's as much as my job's worth," he declared,
with a shake of the head.

" I think not," rejoined Bernard. " Two of us
are police officers."

" That's no news," declared the operator.

A fortnight ago Bradfield and Preston would
have been completely taken aback by this revela-
tion. They weren't now. Their supposed secret
seemed to be common property in Brinkwater.
Not that that mattered now. The work they had
been called upon to perform had been successfully,
though unhappily, accomplished.

" Inspector Protheroe knows what we're asking

you to do," said Phil. " We're hoping to trap a criminal who is indirectly responsible for what happened to Mr. Tankerton."

" A right good sort was Mr. Tankerton," declared the craneman. " More'n once he's done me a good turn. And now something's happened —what I don't rightly know—and he's a dead un. You want me to swing the crane arm across the road? Right: I'm your man!"

The chums between them explained what was required.

" We'll be just across the road to give you the signal," explained Phil. " We can see what's taking place outside Tankerton's house from here and we can stop other cars well in time before they crash into the crane."

They agreed upon how and when the signals for lowering the arm of the crane were to be given. Then, the cheerful smile returning to his face, the operator resumed his decidedly monotonous task.

But, if everything went according to plan, it would be anything but monotonous before the ending of the day.

The four men took up their positions. To any outside observer they looked like ordinary summer visitors, although quite a number of Brinkwater folk knew who three of them were. Fuller was more or less a stranger.

It was now half-past nine. A few cars were passing in either direction, but most traffic kept

to the by-pass recently constructed to avoid con-
gestion in the village's one through-road running
east and west.

Then Phil noticed that Inspector Protheroe,
accompanied by a police sergeant, was approaching.

"Ah, good morning!" he exclaimed affably.
"Let's hope it *is* good morning and won't need
to be good night! I don't know what you think
about it, but I'd much rather make Zensky's
acquaintance in broad daylight than in the dark!"

"Let's hope so, sir," rejoined Preston, who
realized that the inspector was having another
dig at him.

"I've completed my arrangements," continued
Protheroe. "The van is in position in the side
road, ready to close the main road at a moment's
notice. I've a plain clothes constable in the
doorway of the house opposite Tankerton's and
a uniformed man in those bushes by the side of
his house."

The inspector was still describing his plans
when a large limousine appeared coming from
the direction of Dorchester. In the front seat
was a uniformed chauffeur, while the owner—
supposing he was the owner—was reclining on
the rear seat, apparently absorbed in a newspaper.

The car swung past. The sunlight, glinting
on the windows, prevented Protheroe and those
with him from seeing the occupants clearly.

"The car's slowing down!" declared Phil.

" Yes, it's stopping!" added Protheroe. " By Jupiter, it has stopped—outside Tankerton's house!"

It was not exactly a correct statement.

The car, continuing to keep to its proper side of the road, had pulled up opposite the residence of the late manager of the Brinkwater Rope Walk. The chauffeur got out, crossed the roadway and knocked on the front door.

Receiving no reply he knocked a second time. Evidently he hadn't noticed the slight visible damage done by the fire to the front of the house.

Then the plain-clothes constable strolled up and spoke to the chauffeur. Both of them crossed the road. It looked as if the police officer was engaged in an altercation with the owner of the car—a supposition that looked like being confirmed when he gave a loud blast with his whistle.

In less than ten seconds the police van had blocked the road. Out of it tumbled half a dozen beefy constables.

It was almost impossible for the car to get away. The constable who had first challenged the chauffeur was now between him and the limousine. They appeared to be still arguing.

Thinking that it was about time that he had a look in, Inspector Protheroe strode slowly and with a dignified mien towards the car. He was followed by the sergeant, while Bradfield and Preston, accompanied by the representatives of the press, brought up the rear.

That meant that the chums were deserting their allotted posts. In the circumstances they didn't give a thought to that!

" What's all this, Constable Pyke?" demanded the inspector.

" This person, sir," began the policeman, " was acting in a suspicious manner in attempting to enter premises now in the care of the police. He claims to be chauffeur to Sir Montague Corton and that that gentleman is now seated in this vehicle."

The chums could have roared with laughter. Only the realization that they, too, were members of a police force prevented them from expressing spontaneous, unrestrained mirth.

To them the situation was an obvious one.

Sir Montague, totally unaware of his manager's death, had been staying at his London house. While there he had decided to do as he had done on previous occasions—to pay a surprise visit to the Brinkwater Rope Walk.

Finding the place deserted and the main gates locked, the chauffeur, acting upon his master's orders, had driven on to stop outside Tankerton's now deserted house.

" For some reason—the meaning of which is absolutely inexplicable as far as I am concerned —one of your men, inspector, has behaved most unmannerly!" declared the baronet indignantly. " My chauffeur has, on demand, produced both his driving licence and his identity card. Not satisfied with that, the constable declines to admit my identity. I can assure you, and produce proof, that I am Sir Montague Corton, of Haxthorpe Hall, in the County of Yorkshire."

"And might I inquire why you were calling at the house occupied by the late George Tankerton?" asked Protheroe.

"The late George Tankerton," echoed the baronet. "You astound me, Inspector!"

"You aren't the only one to express surprise, Sir Montague," rejoined Protheroe, giving the baronet his title just in case he was the person he professed to be. "But you have not answered my question. Why are you calling at Tankerton's house?"

"Because he is—or, rather, I should have said was—he was the manager of the Brinkwater branch of a company of which I am the managing director."

"Might I ask you to produce proofs of your identity, Sir Montague?" asked Protheroe civilly, although he still had his doubts. There were such things as forged identity cards.

"Certainly!" agreed the baronet.

He drew a small leather case from the inside breast-pocket of his coat and opened the flap. Then a look of mild astonishment appeared upon his face.

"That's remarkable!" he exclaimed. "I thought I had my identity card here. It appears to be missing."

At this juncture Phil thought that it was quite time for him to come to Sir Montague Corton's assistance.

" I can, if necessary, swear to your identity, Sir Montague!" he announced, edging close to the bulky form of Inspector Protheroe as he did so.

The baronet stared at the interrupter of the proceedings. He had a bad memory for faces and a worse one for people's names. In his official capacity he came in contact with dozens of strangers. Generally he had his secretary, Thornebury, to put him right in such instances, but at the moment Thornebury was at Haxthorpe Hall, roughly three hundred miles away.

" Thank you," said Sir Montague. " But I'm afraid that I cannot just place you!"

" You remember Sub-Inspectors Bradfield and Preston calling upon you at Haxthorpe Hall with reference to suspected sabotage at Brinkwater Rope Walk, Sir Montague?"

" Of course! Of course!" agreed the baronet. " It's very good of you to appear at a most opportune moment. And now, Inspector, I trust that your suspicions have vanished."

" Certainly, Sir Montague," agreed Protheroe.

" And tell me, Inspector," continued the now mollified baronet, " what is the meaning of this demonstration in force by the police? And why is all this activity taking place outside Tankerton's house?"

Inspector Protheroe did not reply to either question. He realized that the attempt to arrest Zensky might be seriously jeopardized if that individual took it into his head to arrive earlier than he had been expected. Finding the road blocked, he would abandon his idea of calling upon Tankerton and, posing as a motorist on tour, would brazenly ask the inspector the cause of his delay and how long it would be before the offending vehicle—the police van—was removed!

" Do you mind driving on, Sir Montague?" he asked. " I'll have that van removed at once. You can leave your car on the church green, if you wish, and then walk back here. No doubt Sub-Inspectors Preston and Bradfield can find you a vantage point from which you will have a fairly uninterrupted view of probable impending operations!"

" And what might they be, Inspector?" asked Sir Montague.

" Bradfield and Preston will keep you well informed, Sir Montague. If you'll excuse me, there are urgent matters requiring my immediate attention!"

He went off to give orders for the removal of the obstructing van. The police had already boarded it for the second time that morning. Quite a few of the local inhabitants had collected in an endeavour to find out what all this fuss was about.

In addition four cars had come to involuntary

halts, three from the direction of Bridport and one from that of Dorchester.

To allow a free passage for these vehicles and to get the villagers away from the scene, Protheroe ordered the police van to drive for a distance of about a couple of miles towards Bridport, and then return to its hiding-place in the *cul-de-sac*.

He fervently hoped that Zensky would not arrive before the police trap was set for the second time.

Although Sir Montague raised no objection to Protheroe's suggestion—or was it an order?— that his car should be left on the church green, he had no intention of walking back that distance.

But Bernard and Phil had no wish for the baronet's company at this stage. Already, with the reporter and the press photographer, there would be four men " hanging around " close to the still busy mechanical excavator. Four were quite a sufficient number. Besides, if Zensky should attempt to shoot his way out—an unlikely thing to happen—the baronet *might* stop a stray bullet.

Having given Sir Montague a brief account of the events leading up to Tankerton's decease and the reason for the presence of a considerable number of police, the chums conducted the baronet to the locked gates of the rope-walk and suggested that he should climb over them so that he would be out of sight and possible danger should Zensky show fight.

Sir Montague, who in all probability hadn't scaled a gate since his schooldays, did so. After all, he was on his own property!

Meanwhile Bickerton and Fuller had gone back to their temporary "pitch", close to the place where the mechanical excavator was still pursuing its monotonous though useful task.

"Let's hope you got a good one!" remarked the reporter.

"What exactly do you mean?" asked the press photographer.

"Why, a snap of that baronet fellow having a heated argument with Protheroe!"

"But I didn't take one."

"A bright lad you are!" rejoined Bickerton, with withering scorn. "Why didn't you?"

"I forgot all about my camera when that baronet fellow was arguing with Protheroe," admitted Fuller.

"Well, you've missed one chance although the picture wouldn't be front page news," declared Bickerton. "I didn't bring you along to sit pretty! Jump to it next time, my lad!"

Having deposited Sir Montague Corton out of harm's way—or, rather, they hoped they had—Bernard and Phil rejoined the two press representatives.

They waited, watching the light traffic pass. The mechanical excavator was carrying on with its monotonous task, the smiling driver occasionally giving the "thumbs up" sign to Bradfield and his companions. There wasn't a policeman within sight.

Again the trap had been set.

At length the church clock struck eleven. Zensky had not put in an appearance.

Phil dropped with a bullet through his leg

For the next five minutes the road was deserted as far as wheeled traffic was concerned.

"I hope to goodness the fellow isn't putting off his appearance until eleven to-night," observed Bernard.

Phil shrugged his shoulders.

"I thought that criminals—master criminals in particular—always worked to a time-table," remarked Bickerton, as he lighted his fifth consecutive cigarette.

"On a job, perhaps," conceded Bernard. "But when it comes to fixing up a meeting with a pal they mightn't be so dead on time."

"I remember once——" began Bickerton.

"What's this coming?" interrupted Phil. "Don't all look at once!"

The caution was necessary. A large saloon car was approaching and slowing down. It was neither so big nor so opulent as that of Sir Montague, but it didn't look a poor man's car. The registration plates indicated that it had been put on the road not earlier than the present year.

Again the glinting rays of the sun made it difficult for anyone on the footpath to see clearly what the two occupants looked like. The driver was a thick-set, full-faced man, but, as he was seated, it was difficult to guess his height. His companion appeared to be taller, with square shoulders. He was sitting bolt upright, as if expecting to see someone or something ahead. Part of the broad brim of his hat had been pulled down almost level with his eyes. The rear seats were empty.

As the car swept by, the two occupants turned their heads and glanced, not at the mechanical excavator, but at the group standing on the footpath.

In quite a casual manner Phil looked the other way. His companions, notwithstanding their curiosity, had kept themselves well under control. They might have been discussing the prospects of the Brinkwater cricket team in their forth-coming match with their Copton rivals.

Although the car had slowed down it didn't stop outside Tankerton's house. " That's not our man!" declared Bernard disappointedly.

The car continued in the direction of Bridport. Then it appeared to be about to turn to the left, into the *cul-de-sac* where the police van and its uniformed inmates were waiting. Then, evidently finding that road blocked, it swerved back into the main road and was lost to sight round a bend.

" That's the fellow!" declared Phil. " He was going to turn until he saw the van!"

" Let's hope he didn't spot any of the police

in it," added Bernard. " If so, he's off for all he's worth."

" I don't think he has," said Bickerton. " If that had been the case the police van would be after him by this time!"

A couple of long-drawn-out minutes passed—more than sufficient for the police in ambush to start up their vehicle and enough for the powerful car to travel more than a mile in the direction of Bridport.

" If that's Zensky, it's the last we've seen of him to-day," declared Bernard. " You've lost your one chance of getting a snap of him, Fuller!"

" I'm afraid so," admitted the press photographer. " Monday always is my unlucky day!"

" The car's coming back!" announced Phil excitedly. " Yes! I think it is!—I don't know, though!"

" Yes, it is," declared Bernard. " Or if it isn't, it's a twin brother!"

" Aren't you warning the craneman?" asked Bickerton.

" No!" replied Bradfield.

There wasn't time for him to explain his refusal. In spite of the car's suspicious movements, there was little or nothing else it had done to justify the blocking of the road by the arm of the crane. The driver had not as yet been challenged.

" It's stopping outside Tankerton's house," exclaimed Phil.

Obviously that was the driver's intention. Why

he had originally driven past the house was something of a puzzle, unless it was his intention to
drive off in the direction of Dorchester at the
conclusion of his anticipated interview or at the
first sign of anything of a suspicious nature.

The car stopped.

Bernard and his companions could see the
passenger leaning back, apparently with the object
of handling a case of some sort lying on one of the
rear seats. The driver remained without attempting to alight.

He sounded his horn—two gentle toots.

He waited about a minute and then sounded
the klaxon again.

If he expected to see Tankerton open the front
door he was mistaken.

Instead a uniformed police constable appeared
from the side of the building and made as if he
were about to cross the road in front of the
stationary vehicle. He was taking slow measured
steps and refraining from giving more than a glance
at the car, his object apparently being to avoid
suspicion on the part of its occupants.

Then, turning quickly, he challenged the
driver—at least it seemed to the chums that was
what he was doing. No doubt he was asking the
driver for his licence.

A moment later the constable reeled backwards
with both hands clapped to his face.

Zensky—for it was he—had fired a pistol at
point-blank range.

There was no report. The weapon might have been an automatic fitted with a silencer.

It wasn't. Actually it was a water-pistol, which on this occasion had discharged a jet of liquid ammonia.

For the present the luckless constable was *hors de combat*. Whether he would be blinded for life was something that remained to be seen. Although suffering agonies, he groped for his whistle, found it, placed it between his lips and gave a shrill blast.

Already other police were making for the car. Led by Inspector Protheroe they poured out of the *cul-de-sac*. Unfortunately they were well behind the car. The inspector's disposition of his men had been at fault. Only the chums' road-block—to which he had given a grudging consent—lay between Zensky and a way of escape.

Bernard did not wait for the car to be set in motion.

"Swing the crane round and lower it!" he shouted to the now alert driver.

Without a moment's hesitation the cheerful-faced fellow manipulated the required levers. The crane, with a filled bucket of slush suspended from its extremity, swung across the road. At the same time the long metal arm began to drop to form an impassable barrier to every form of wheeled traffic.

By now Zensky's car was in motion.

The driver, mistakenly imagining that the pursuing police would pour a murderous fusillade into the back of the car—and, perhaps, deprive him of any need for a driving licence—crouched over his steering wheel.

There were reports, but not from the policemen's firearms. They were not carrying any.

Zensky, who had climbed into the back of the car, had smashed the rear window and was firing more or less blindly at his blue-uniformed pursuers.

Now the car was within twenty yards of the spot where Bradfield and his companions were standing. Between them and the car was the still slowly descending arm of the crane.

Zensky's driver had also seen it.

He throttled back and applied his brakes. Then, thinking that there was still sufficient clearance, he accelerated.

Then there was a terrific crash.

There was sufficient room for the car to tear under the jib of the crane, but the driver hadn't taken into account the heavy iron bucket.

The four men ran for their lives.

It was just as well they did.

The car, with most of its off-side ripped off— the luckless driver being killed instantly in the process—careered violently to the left, coming to a standstill with its bonnet telescoped against a stone wall.

Then, to the astonishment of Bernard and his companions, the man they now knew to be

Zensky jumped clear of the wreckage. There was blood on his face, but evidently his physical powers were not impaired.

Brandishing his automatic he ran in their direction, evidently thinking that four civilians were far less of a danger to him than the pursuing police constables.

Bernard and Phil—true to their air police training and tradition—stood alert to make a flying grapple at the desperado. Bickerton and Fuller didn't. Wisely they decided that it wasn't the part of a newspaper's employees to tackle an armed criminal.

The photographer threw himself flat, the back of his head and body pressing against the wall, while the reporter crouched close to him. He didn't want to be involved, although he was determined to see what was taking place.

A shot rang out.

Giving a yelp of pain, Bickerton clasped his left arm above the elbow.

Almost at once there was another report, and Phil dropped with a bullet through his leg just above the knee.

That left Bernard.

Unhesitatingly he made to grapple with his antagonist. Before he could do so, Zensky pressed the trigger of his automatic.

There was a click, but no report.

Either the cartridge was defective or he had emptied the magazine.

With a snarl of rage Zensky hurled the empty pistol at Bernard's head.

It would have inflicted a nasty wound and perhaps have knocked him senseless had Bernard not ducked. The weapon just missed the top of his skull, whipping of his cap as it did so.

In his effort to dodge the flying missile Bernard was temporarily thrown off his balance. In a second his antagonist, quick to take every advantage, had slipped past him and had taken to his heels.

It looked as if Zensky had an even chance to effect his escape—at least for the present.

There were police in pursuit but they were a good distance behind. The crane, that had put paid to Zensky's car, was no longer an aid. It was a hindrance. Until it could be removed—the bucket was still mixed up with the wreckage—no other vehicle could pass. Consequently the police were obliged to continue the chase on foot.

Resisting his first impulse to go to the assistance of his wounded chum, Bradfield started in pursuit of the fugitive. At all costs he must get his man!

For all he knew Phil might be dangerously wounded. Perhaps he was already dead!

Yes, at all costs he, Bradfield, must get his man!

In spite of being shaken when his car was wrecked, Zensky was running strongly. Bernard had all his work cut out to maintain his distance. None of the pursuing police was able to decrease the gap between them and the fugitive.

As he was about to run past Sea View—Bernard wondered whether he'd attempt to hide there— Jasper Nightingale, followed by Mrs. Marshbarrow carrying a mop, came out of the front gate.

Bernard shouted to them to go back. The warning was either unheard or disregarded. Zensky made a slight detour in order to avoid them. As he did so, Mrs. Marshbarrow hurled her mop at him. It struck the road just in front of him. He could have jumped it with ease.

For some unknown reason he didn't. With one foot just in front of the handle and one close behind he tripped and measured his length on the ground.

Catching up with the prostrate man, Bradfield waited. If necessary he could grapple with him, but Zensky was making no effort to regain his feet.

Bernard carried no handcuffs. The police, the

nearest now only twenty yards away, could remedy that deficiency.

Suddenly Zensky began to writhe.

Turning him over on his back, Bernard pulled the man's hand from his mouth.

It was too late.

Beaten and cornered and knowing that he was for the gallows should any of his shots have had a fatal effect, Zensky had gone to his last resort. He had taken a tablet of poison, the result of which had been almost instantaneous.

Leaving the local police to deal with the body, Bernard, though considerably winded, hurried back to the spot where he had left his wounded chum.

In spite of his anxiety—for both Phil and Bickerton might have been seriously injured, perhaps fatally—Bernard could not help experiencing a peculiar sense of elation. He had got his man, although not in the manner he had anticipated. And since Zensky was dead there wouldn't be a case at the Assizes involving him. At most Bernard would have to attend two inquests—one on Zensky's unhappy dupe, George Tankerton.

Bernard hadn't gone far when he saw Bickerton and Fuller coming in his direction. The reporter's face looked grey and drawn. The left sleeve of his coat showed sinister stains.

" Where's Preston?" asked his chum anxiously.

" Back there," replied Bickerton vaguely. " A First Aid man's fixing him up."

" And you?"

" A mere nothing," declared the reporter.
" Left arm—that won't prevent me carrying on.
What's happened to Zensky—lost him?"

" In a way, yes," replied Bradfield. " He took
a dose of poison—and I was fool enough to let
him do it!"

" More copy!" declared Bickerton. " We'll
go along."

" But that bullet wound?"

" Can wait! Come along, Fuller! But half a
minute, Bradfield. I take it all back what I said
about Fuller a short while ago! He's turned up
trumps. While I was cowering against the wall,
he took four snaps of Zensky as he was blazing
away and when he hurled his pistol at you.
They'll be pictures taken at an unusual angle—
at ground level—but Fuller took them: didn't
you, boy? When we're finished up there "—
indicating the scene of Zensky's final act—" we're
making for Dorchester as fast as my old bus can
take us. Those pictures must appear in to-day's
editions of the *Evening Monitor*. Well, cheerio
once more!"

" Who'd be a pressman?" thought Bernard, as
he continued on the way towards the village.
" Williamson wasn't far out when he said he
hoped Bickerton would prove to be a better
reporter than he was as an airman!"

The jib of the crane had been swung clear by
the time Bernard returned. The wreckage of

Zensky's car still remained, but the body of its driver had been taken away. A constable was standing by, controlling the renewed flow of traffic.

"Nothing to worry about, sir," he replied, in answer to Bradfield's inquiry. "They've taken Mr. Preston to the Crab and Lobster. But what's happened to Zensky, sir? Has he got away?"

"He's gone to the bourne from which no one returns, constable," replied Bernard.

"What; have they taken him to Bournemouth?" asked the perplexed policeman. "For why? That's outside the county of Dorset!"

Bernard could not conceal a smile as he enlightened the man. Then he made his way to Brinkwater's one and only inn.

He found Phil reclining on a sofa. A rug covered his body from the waist downwards. Unlike Bickerton's, his face wasn't noticeably pale. He gave his chum a cheery smile.

"Have they got Zensky?" was the first question.

"And how goes it with you?" asked Bernard, after he had satisfied his thirst for knowledge upon the subject of the dead arch-saboteur.

"Quite all right. I didn't think that a bullet wound through the fleshy part of my leg could be so painful. It felt as if I'd been kicked by a mule! The bullet went clean through; so I haven't to bother about that. The wound doesn't hurt now—or very little. I should be quite all right in a week's time."

A doctor arrived soon after.

An examination showed that the First Aid constable who had attended to Phil's injury, had done his work efficiently. The doctor was quite satisfied about that.

"We'll have you in our cottage hospital," he added. "You should be discharged cured by next Monday," which confirmed Phil's statement to a day.

"You did a smart piece of work with that mop of yours, Mrs. Marshbarrow," observed Bernard, as he sat down to his solitary evening meal.

"That's nothing," declared the proprietress of Sea View modestly. "I've knocked over a few rats in my time with my mop, but never such a big un before— Will you be stopping on, Mr. Bradfield, until Mr. Preston comes out of 'orspital?"

Bernard did. It was a fairly hectic week. Sir Montague Corton called to see him and to express his thanks for having freed the Brinkwater Rope Walk from the pestilent disease of sabotage.

Then there were the inquests, held for no apparent reason on two consecutive days.

At the one on Tankerton, no mention was made of his connection with the blackmailing Zensky, and a verdict of Accidental Death was returned. In the case of Zensky, outside witnesses, some from Scotland Yard, brought ample evidence of his subversive activities. A verdict of *felo de se* was unanimously returned.

On the following Monday morning, Phil was discharged from hospital. During the afternoon H.104 was flown from Bere Regis Aerodrome by one of Mr. Williamson's pilots.

The next day Bernard, with Phil as passenger, flew back to Hawkscar.

" Good show!" declared Chief Inspector Colin Standish, after they had made their report, though most of the details were by this time in his possession through other sources. " I suppose both of you are ready for fourteen days' leave."

" Thanks awfully, sir!" exclaimed the two sub-inspectors simultaneously.

" Then clear off and have a thundering good time," continued Colin Standish. " But bear in mind: when you return to duty I've another case —an interesting one—waiting for you!"